Harrowing Ascent of Half Dome

Yosemite is awesome!
Mike
Aug 08

Mike Graf

Illustrated by
Marjorie Leggitt

FULCRUM

Adventures with the Parkers: **YOSEMITE**

3

Text © 2007 Mike Graf
Illustrations © 2007 Marjorie Leggitt
Photographs: © Mike Graf: 1, 23, 30, 32, 46, 55
(bottom), 57, 60, 70, 74, 78, 87, 91
© Shutterstock: Cover, title page, 6, 11, 14, 15,
19, 26, 27, 28, 35, 42, 43, 47, 48, 50, 51, 52, 55
(top), 58, 61, 62, 67, 68–69, 82, 83, 89, 90,
94–95
© IndexOpen: 31, 33
© JupiterImages: 37
Map courtesy of the National Park Service
Yosemite Decimal System chart used by permis-
sion of www.climber.org/data/decimal.html.

Printed in China by P. Chan & Edward, Inc.
0 9 8 7 6 5 4 3 2 1

Editorial: Faith Marcovecchio, Carolyn Sobczak
Design: Ann W. Douden
Cover image: Marjorie Leggitt
Models for twins: Amanda and Ben Frazier

Library of Congress Cataloging-in-Publication
Data

Graf, Mike.
  Yosemite : harrowing ascent of Half Dome / by
Mike Graf ; illustrations by Marjorie Leggitt.
    p. cm. -- (Adventures with the Parkers)
  Summary: Twin brother and sister, James and
Morgan, embark on another adventure with their
parents to explore the history, unusual geology,
famous sites, plants, and animals of Yosemite
National Park. Sidebar notes contain additional
facts about the area and describe the park's regu-
lations and tourist facilities.
  ISBN 978-1-55591-609-1 (pbk.)
  1. Yosemite National Park (Calif.)--Fiction. [1.
Yosemite National Park (Calif.)--Fiction. 2.
National parks and reserves--Fiction. 3. Hiking--
Fiction. 4. Vacations--Fiction. 5. Family
life--Fiction.] I. Leggitt, Marjorie C., ill. II. Title.
PZ7.G751574 Yo 2007
[Fic]--dc22

2006038237

FULCRUM PUBLISHING
4690 Table Mountain Drive, Suite 100
800-992-2908 • 303-277-1623
www.fulcrumbooks.com

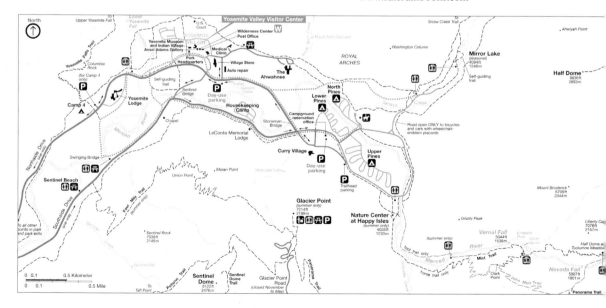

James balanced his feet on a narrow ledge.

He waited there while Mike, a climbing guide from the Yosemite Mountaineering School, anchored in above him.

James looked down from his perch on the side of Ranger Rock. In the parking lot far below, he could see two tiny dots that he knew were his parents. *I bet they're sitting there reading,* James thought.

James's twin sister, Morgan, had just finished her climb and was waiting above. James turned to look at the pile of rope that lay coiled on a flat rock next to him. The pile grew smaller and smaller as Mike pulled up the excess.

There was another climber just a few feet away. He was being guided up the rock by a woman. The woman was anchored in above the climber, waiting for him to reach her.

"Is this your first time up here?" the climber asked James.

"Yes," James answered.

"Well, you're doing great," the climber said. "Not a lot of

people your age even try to get this far. And here you are, over 700 feet off the ground!"

"Is that how high I am?" James asked. He moved closer to the cliff and held on tighter.

James watched the other climber. Instead of going up the rock using his arms and legs, he was pulling himself up a rope. And, his equipment was different. His legs were covered by a protective cloth, and they dangled limply to the side. The climber's rope was attached to his body, but a bar was connected to the rope above his waist. The climber pushed the bar up the rope and then pulled himself six inches higher.

"This is just my way of getting up the mountain," the climber explained.

"I was told to mostly use my legs," James said.

"Except when your legs don't work," the climber replied. "Then you can use your arms with a pull-up bar, like this."

Suddenly, the rope pulled tight on James's harness.

"That's me!" James called up to Mike.

"You're on belay!" Mike called down.

"Climbing!" James responded.

"Climb on!" Mike answered.

James looked up. Mike was already at the top of Ranger Rock. He was sitting next to Morgan, who was peering over the cliff with her camera.

"Well, here goes," James announced.

"Good luck," the other climber said. "By the way, my name is Mark, and that's Kimberly up there."

Kimberly waved at James. "Hello."

"Hi," James replied. "It's nice to meet both of you. I'm James."

James felt the rope pulling on him again.

"Climb on!" Mike hollered down. "I've got you."

COMMON CLIMBING TERMS

ANCHOR   A place on the rock where several pieces of gear securely attach the climber to the rock.

BELAY   A place on the rock where the rope is secured. To belay is also to feed rope for the climber and to hold the rope to brake a partner's fall.

GEAR   A general term for protection devices or equipment placed in the rock and meant to keep the lead climber from falling to the ground. Gear is also anything brought for the climb.

OVERHANG   Where the rock juts out at more than a 90-degree angle so that the climber has to climb with his back facing the ground for a short distance.

PITCH   The stretch of rock between anchors along a rope. A rope length is typically 60 meters (197 feet).

PROTECTION   Devices used by a climber to secure the rope to the rock and stop a fall.

RAPPEL   A controlled way of descending, or going down, the rope.

SLACK   To give a climber slack means to feed the climber more rope to climb with, loosening your hold on the rope.

SMEAR   A foothold where as much of the sole of the foot as possible is pressed into the rock.

James took a step. He wedged his left foot into a tiny crack. Then he smeared his right foot onto a lower-angled spot on the rock. James put his hands into a crack and thrust his body upward. He felt Mike pull the rope tight.

"I'm on the last pitch on Ranger Rock," James muttered to himself. "I hope I can make it."

"Trust the rope and keep the weight over your feet," instructed Mark, who was to the left of James. Mark did several more pull-ups with his bar. He started shifting over to a different side of the rock. "I'm like Tu-tok-a-na the inchworm," Mark said. "I climb up just inches at a time."

THE MIWOK LEGEND OF TU-TOK-A-NU'-LA

Two bear cubs lived in the Ah-wah-nee Valley. One day, they went swimming. After playing in the water, they both climbed up onto a large boulder to dry off in the sun. Soon, they fell asleep.

The bear cubs slept long and hard. Many days and nights went by. Still, they slept on the rock.

After many moons, the rock rose to great heights. It lifted into the sky, out of sight of all the animals below. The top of the rock scraped against the moon. Still, the two bear cubs slept.

On the ground below, the birds and animals missed the two bear cubs and cried out for them. One at a time, each animal tried to work its way up the cliff. First the mouse climbed. Then the rat, raccoon, grizzly bear, and even the mountain lion tried. All of the animals fell back to the ground. They couldn't climb the massive rock to get to the sleeping bears.

Tu-tok-a-na the inchworm crept up the rock. Inch by inch he measured and wormed his way up cracks, around overhangs, over rock holds, and across ledges. Soon, the inchworm had climbed farther than any of the other animals. He inched his way out of sight.

Finally, Tu-tok-a-na worked his way to the top. He scooped up the two bear cubs and climbed down with them.

Tu-tok-a-na continued to climb after this. The inchworm climbed all over the cliffs of Yosemite.

CALLING YOSEMITE HOME

The first people to live in Yosemite Valley were there about 6,000 years ago. In the mid-1800s, the Miwok Indians inhabited Yosemite Valley. They called the valley *Awahnee*, which means "place of the gaping mouth." These Indians called themselves Awahneechee. They ate acorns and hunted and fished throughout the valley. There are Native American sites in the valley today, as well as a replicated Indian village and a museum for visitors to see.

James watched Mark for a moment and then climbed on. He took a small step and then another. Then James used his hands to hold himself steady.

"Keep your bottom out!" Morgan directed from above.

"Got it," James answered. He pushed and pulled his body up a few more feet and then balanced himself on a ledge. James was now thirty feet above the last place where he was anchored in and about thirty feet below Morgan and Mike.

But the hardest part, the crux, was still above him. It was a short, straight cliff with few places to grab on to, followed by an overhang. Morgan had cruised up it. *Maybe that's because she weighs less*, James reasoned.

James looked up. He studied the rock to find his next move. He felt like he was looking at the pieces of a giant jigsaw puzzle. He was searching for a way to complete the big picture.

James reached for a tiny handhold and fumbled around for a good grip. He extended himself on his tiptoes. But his feet started to shake. James took a deep breath and tried to calm himself.

"You can do it!" he heard Morgan call out.

"I hope so," James whispered back.

"I've got you," Mike said calmly.

"Here goes!" James called out. He lunged upward, moving his hands first, then his feet. James gripped the rock with one hand, and then the other. He tried to smear his foot onto a tiny ledge.

"Ahh!" James cried out. He lost his grip and fell several feet into the air. James caromed into the cliff and dangled from the rope, high above Yosemite Valley. He kicked his feet into the wall and stopped himself from smacking into the cliff again. James shook out his arms. "Man, that was hard."

James looked up at Mike and Morgan, who were perched above him. Morgan snapped a picture of James hanging by the rope. "I don't know if I can make it," James called out.

"I know you can," Morgan encouraged him.

"What's this rated?" James asked Mike.

"The overhang route is a 5.8," Mike answered.

"Who came up with these routes?" Morgan asked as she looked down at her brother.

The world's largest piece of granite

"The first people who climbed them," Mike answered. "And those people got to name them." Mike pointed at a massive straight-edged mountain to the west. "See that over there? That's one of Yosemite's most famous rocks, El Capitan.

A man named Warren Harding was the first person to climb it, in 1958. One of his routes was called The Nose. It took him forty-five days to complete it."

"It takes that long?" James asked.

"It depends on which route you take," Mike explained. "It took early climbers like Harding a lot longer, because they had to put in all the bolts, which are up there permanently, and pieces of protection. But now, it usually takes around three to four days to complete, although some routes can be completed in one long day."

"I hope I'm not up here that long," James said. He tried to grab on to the rock, but his legs started shaking again and he lost his grip. James dangled in the air. He swallowed nervously.

HOW HARD IS THIS ROCK?

Climbing is rated according to difficulty. The most common rating system used in the United States is the Yosemite Decimal System, developed by Royal Robbins in the late 1950s. It rates climbs between 5.0 and 5.11 and higher. Later, the Sierra Club added the 1 to 6 scale for all mountaineering.

Class 1   Walking

Class 2   Hiking in terrain

Class 3   Rock scrambling at a steep angle

Class 4   A rope may be necessary; falls can be fatal

Class 5   Technical rock climbing; equipment is always used, falls can be fatal

Class 5 ratings begin at 5.0 and go up to 5.11 and beyond. Class 5 rock climbs vary in difficulty due to steepness, type of rock, how many cracks or holds there are, and overhangs along the route. Ratings also are given due to the "crux," or hardest move on that route.

Class 6   Direct aid climbing; equipment used for upward body progress. Equipment absorbs body weight.

"I don't think I can make it!" James called up.

"You can do it!" Morgan replied. She shifted her body to take a picture, accidentally kicking a small rock loose. It tumbled down the cliff.

"Rock!" Morgan screamed.

For an instant that seemed like a lifetime, Morgan watched the rock gather momentum. It was headed right toward her brother.

"James!" Morgan shouted.

James looked up. He saw the rock careening toward him. James shut his eyes and jerked his body sideways. The rock glanced off James's helmet and broke into several smaller pieces. Rock debris and dust continued showering down Ranger Rock.

James opened his eyes. "Rock!" he screamed to any climbers who might be below him. James watched as the rock debris disappeared.

"I'm so sorry," Morgan said.

"I'm okay," James replied. "Thanks to this helmet."

James took a deep breath and tried to grab on again. Both his hands and feet lost their grip. Again, James dangled from his rope while he tapped against the cliff. After a moment, he lifted his arms, then quickly put them back down. "My arms are tired," he called out. "I give up!"

James looked over at Mark on another part of the cliff. Mark thrust his bar up six inches, and then pulled himself up his rope. Mark repeated this over and over again.

With renewed energy, James tried again. He hoisted himself up to a handhold, but stayed there. "I'm stuck."

"Wait here on the flat area of the summit," Mike said to Morgan. "And stay anchored in. Don't untie anything."

"Okay," Morgan agreed.

Mike worked with his ropes for a moment. "I'll be right there," he called down to James.

Mike lowered himself until he hung next to James. "You look okay," Mike said. "I don't see any cuts or bruises. You were lucky."

Rock climbing in Yosemite began with John Muir in the late 1800s. Muir is often called the "father of the national parks," and he was an original leader of the Sierra Club, an organization dedicated to preserving beautiful, natural places. Muir particularly loved Yosemite and the Sierra Nevada, which he called "a special temple of nature and an immense hall flanked by granite cliffs and thundering waterfalls." When he first came to Yosemite, Muir described it as "the unforgettable skyline of sculptured domes and spires." Muir climbed many of the area's peaks without the help of the technical equipment used today.

Modern climbing techniques began being used in the 1930s. The first climb of Washington Column in Yosemite was in 1933. Cathedral Spire was climbed in 1934. World War II temporarily delayed the increased popularity of the sport. But from 1947 until 1970, rock climbing became very popular in the park. Two famous climbing pioneers were Warren Harding and Royal Robbins. Harding and Robbins led the first ascents, or climbs, up many of Yosemite's big walls, including Half Dome in 1957 and El Capitan in 1958.

During this time, many climbers from all over the world, including Harding and Robbins, gathered at a specific walk-in campsite in Yosemite Valley to share stories and information about climbing and the climbing routes they took. It's called Camp 4.

James rubbed his arm across his forehead and wiped off beads of sweat. "I can't lift my arms anymore. I feel like I've been doing hundreds of pull-ups."

"That's how Mark gets up these rocks," Mike stated. "He was hurt in a climbing accident several years ago and lost the use of his legs," he explained. "Do you want some help?"

"You mean you're going to rescue me?" James asked. "How would you get me off of here? With a helicopter?"

Mike laughed. "No. I don't mean that at all. I think you can make it to the top yourself. Would you like me to tell you where the good footholds are?"

"Okay," James said. "But I'm not so sure I can make it."

"You'll be fine," Mike said. "Just focus on your feet. See that little knob of rock above your knee? Get your left foot there. Then reach up to that crack above your shoulder with your right hand."

James did what Mike said. Then he moved his right foot up. Suddenly, like an inchworm, he was crawling up the rock.

"Great job, James!" Morgan called down.

Quickly, James moved up to just below the overhang. Mike followed.

"That was better," James said. He looked up. "But how am I supposed to get over that?"

"Reach out to the right as far as you can," Mike suggested. "Grab on with your hand and then swing your leg over in one quick move."

"You can do it!" Morgan called out.

James looked up at his sister. Morgan was peering over the top of the rock just above him. "You don't have to shout now. I'm only ten feet away."

James took a deep breath. He lunged at the handhold to grab it, but slipped back again. For a moment, James felt like he was dangling upside down in the air. "Whoa!" he said. "That's not exactly the position I want to be in!" He lunged at the rock again. This time, he grabbed on. James slung his right leg over to a protruding point.

"Keep going!" Mike called out.

"I can't!" James said. His legs were shaking wildly.

James grunted while doing a one-handed pull-up. He slowly lifted himself. James swung his other leg over and kicked it around until he found a good foothold. Using both his feet, James pushed himself up and slithered over the top of the cliff. He crawled forward, away from the edge.

"Welcome to the top of Ranger Rock!" Morgan greeted her brother.

Morgan took a picture of James and then gave him a high five.

James crawled forward a few more feet and collapsed onto his stomach next to the anchor. He lay still for a moment. "I didn't think I was going to make it."

Morgan looked at her brother sprawled out on the ground. "You look like our new puppy after a long, hard day."

James turned over and glanced at Morgan. "Maybe we can name him Ranger, after the rock we just climbed." A second later, James sat up. "It's nice to be on solid ground again."

James and Morgan looked at the other anchor on top of the cliff. It was attached to Mark's rope. The rope was quivering back and forth as Mark climbed.

Kimberly, who had climbed ahead of Mark and placed in the protection, sat next to the anchor and waited for him.

James gave Kimberly a puzzled look. "That pull-up bar automatically locks in," Kimberly explained. "He can belay himself."

"Take a look around now that you are on top of the rock," Mike suggested to the twins. "But for now, I am going to keep you anchored in."

Morgan and James looked out at Yosemite Valley. They could see the sheer cliffs of the Cathedral Rocks and the Three Brothers across from them. El Capitan, the world's largest piece of granite, was to the west. To the east was Half Dome—a gigantic round rock that looked like it was sliced in half.

James looked down. He saw their car and a white truck with a green cylinder-shaped trailer on the back. "What's that truck for?"

"That's a bear trap," Mike answered. "We've had a problem bear in this area."

A moment later, Mark reached the top of Ranger Rock. He pulled himself forward until he was next to James and Morgan. Using his arms, Mark scooted across to his anchor, and then, while sitting down, he started undoing his rope.

"Nice climbing!" Mark said to James. "And, good job ducking away from that falling rock."

"Thanks," James said. "By the way, this is my sister, Morgan."

"Hi, Morgan," Mark said.

Mike walked over to Mark. "Hey there, Mark, are you all set for the Half Dome climb?"

"All systems are go," Mark replied. "I'll meet you and the crew on Saturday at the Happy Isles trailhead."

"You got it!" Mike answered.

"I wish I could be there with you," Kimberly said. "But I will be there in spirit."

James walked over to Mike and held still for a moment while Mike undid the anchors.

"We're climbing Half Dome in a few days too," James said to

Mark. "Up the cable route."

"Maybe we'll see you up there," Morgan added.

"Maybe," Mark replied. "But it's hard to know exactly when we'll get to the top. That is one long, difficult cliff to climb."

"Are you ready to go down?" Mike asked.

"Yeah, but how?" Morgan asked. "You've got everything packed up."

Mike smiled. "The other way. Down a trail off the back side of this rock. It's steep, but we can hike it."

"See you later," James said to Mark.

"Take care, James," Mark responded. "I hope to see you climbing again someday."

Mike led Morgan and James to a small, faint trail.

"You mean we could have walked up here?" Morgan asked Mike.

"I'm glad we climbed instead," James said.

After some scrambling down a rocky, steep trail, they made it to the valley floor. They walked around a large boulder and saw their parents.

"Hi!" Morgan called out.

Their mom, Kristen, looked up from her photography book about Ansel Adams. "Welcome back!" she said. "How was it?"

"Great," James answered. "You wouldn't believe the view."

Bob, their dad, closed his book of wilderness essays by John Muir and looked at Morgan and James. "We were able to watch you for a while. But after your second pitch, you were out of our sight. That was some tough climbing you did, though. Are you up for getting nice and cool now?"

"You bet!" James answered.

A few minutes later, Morgan, James, Mom, and Dad headed toward Curry Village to rent a raft for a float trip on the Merced River.

Harrowing Ascent of Half Dome
YOSEMITE

Morgan lay in her sleeping bag with her eyes closed.

She thought back to the rafting trip her family had taken that afternoon on the Merced River, which meanders through Yosemite Valley. It was so peaceful, she remembered. At one point, the family pulled the raft over to a sandbar and rested in the shade by the river. Mom and Dad had brought their books and read while she and James tried to go into the water, but it was too cold.

"Grunt. Grunt. Huff!"

Morgan opened her eyes. It was dark in her tent. She turned over and remembered that she was alone. Morgan listened intently. Something was outside her tent.

"Huff!"

This time, crunching footsteps followed the loud sound.

Morgan's heart beat wildly.

The footsteps grew louder. Whatever was outside was moving closer.

"Huff! Huff!"

It sounded like two giant sneezes, followed by crunching footsteps.

Morgan kept as still as she could. Something brushed against the side of her tent, pressing it inward. Morgan slid to the other side of the tent. The tent popped back out as the footsteps moved away. Morgan tried to calm her breathing down.

The creature outside was clawing around and huffing as if it was searching for something.

"Mom. Dad," Morgan whispered. "James. Are you awake?"

Nobody responded.

"Mom? Dad?" Morgan repeated.

The footsteps grew louder. Morgan peered out through her tent's window. The campground was dark. She moved closer to the window and pressed her nose against the mesh. Morgan froze. She was looking into the shiny, dark eye of a large animal. And it was looking at her!

Morgan jumped back.

The animal grunted and moved away.

Morgan fumbled around for her headlamp. She slipped it on her head, switched it on, and shone it out the window. The large, furry animal paused and looked toward Morgan's light. "A bear!" she whispered. The bear had a shiny yellow tag clipped to its ear. It headed toward James's tent.

Morgan followed the bear with the beam of light.

"Get away from there!" Morgan called out.

The bear glanced back at Morgan and walked away from James's tent. It passed by Mom and Dad's tent and walked between the picnic table and campfire ring.

"A bear in Yosemite Valley," Morgan said to herself. "And on our first night in camp!"

Morgan watched the bear trudge farther away. "James! Mom and Dad!" she whispered urgently. But they didn't answer. *Mom and Dad must be tired after the long drive*, Morgan thought. *And James always sleeps so deeply.*

The bear was now in the next campsite. It walked up to the picnic table and stood up against it with its front feet. The bear lowered its nose into a box on the table and smelled something. Then it scratched a package with its paw. The package ripped open. Morgan saw a bunch of puffy marshmallows tumble to the ground.

Morgan continued watching the bear. The bear shoved its nose into the package. It bit into a bunch of marshmallows and chewed them all at once. Several more dropped to the ground.

Morgan heard a scratching sound coming from the nearby trees. The bear looked toward the sound. A second later, a small bear trotted toward the large bear. It looked up at its mom, and then it started eating the marshmallows on the ground.

"It has a cub!" Morgan whispered. She watched the two bears. The cub put its paw down on several marshmallows and yanked on them with its teeth. Morgan saw some lights flickering in the distance. She heard footsteps coming closer.

The bears looked up from their feast and turned toward the sounds. The cub trotted away into the woods.

"Over here!" one person exclaimed.

"I'm going to get it," the other person said.

Morgan turned toward the voices and saw two people dressed in ranger uniforms. One person shone a light on the bear. The other person pointed a pistol at it.

What? Morgan thought. She wanted to jump out of her tent and scream, "Stop!"

Crack!

The gun went off. It was too late.

The bear was hit. It jumped down from the table and shook its head.

The person fired the gun again.

The bear raced into the forest.

Morgan flew out of her tent and bumped into James, who was rushing out of his tent too. Morgan and James ran to their parents' tent and quickly got inside. The family looked out of the window. They watched the people with the light and pistol walk into the forest, following the two bears.

Morgan leaned against her mother. "I can't believe they shot the bear."

"It looked like it was more scared than hurt," Dad commented. "I wonder why rangers would do that, though."

FOOD FOR THOUGHT

Starting in the 1940s, leftover food in Yosemite Valley was dumped into open garbage bins. This attracted bears, and people gathered around the bins to watch them. This was bad for the bears and the people. Bears sought food from people, which often led to injuries or property damage. This practice stopped in 1971. Now all food and odorous items not in use must be stored in bear-proof lockers located throughout the park.

The family piled out of the car at the Giant Sequoia Grove parking lot.

They stood and looked at the massive trees with reddish brown bark scattered throughout the area.

"Sequoia forests are amazing," Mom commented. "They look so primeval. Almost like dinosaurs could have lived in here."

"Have you seen a sequoia before?" James asked.

"Yes, but in Sequoia National Park, not here," Mom replied.

GROVES OF SEQUOIA

There are sixty-seven sequoia groves left in the world. All of them are in California's Sierra Nevada mountains. Yosemite National Park has three of these groves. They are the Mariposa, Merced, and Tuolumne. The Mariposa Grove is the largest of Yosemite's sequoia groves. It has a museum and holds guided tours. The Mariposa Grove also contains the Grizzly Giant, one of the world's biggest trees.

The family walked quietly through the grove. They could hear their footsteps crunching on cones and needles along the trail. The trail passed by a trickling stream, clumps of ferns, and baby sequoias. Morgan, James, Mom, and Dad circled widely around the largest sequoia in the grove, the Grizzly Giant. The family stopped to admire it.

ELEPHANTINE EVERGREEN

Sequoias and redwoods are the two largest living things on Earth. Both grow in California. While redwoods are sometimes taller—up to 370 feet—sequoias are more bulky. A mature giant sequoia can grow to 310 feet high but weighs the equivalent of forty-six adult male elephants. The tallest tree in the Mariposa Grove is 290 feet tall. The Grizzly Giant is 209 feet. Giant sequoias are found along the western slopes of the Sierra Nevada mountains in California. Redwoods grow near the coast from Monterey, California, to southern Oregon. Sequoias have cones shaped like chicken eggs. Redwood cones are olive shaped.

"Now that's a giant sequoia," Dad commented.

Morgan started taking pictures. "It's got monsterlike branches."

"They look like tentacles sticking out of an octopus," James added. "And they're so high off the ground."

James, Mom, and Dad stood at the fence in front of the Grizzly Giant. Morgan set the automatic timer on her camera. Then she ran over to join her family.

Click! The camera took the picture.

"I'll bet we'll look like toothpicks in the photo compared to that tree," James said.

"But I couldn't get the whole tree in the picture," Morgan said.

Dad joked, "I'm sure *I* didn't look like a toothpick."

"You're still thinking about that sign up at the museum," Mom said, grinning.

"Yep. 'Sequoias are like people,'" Dad said. "'After a while, they stop growing taller, and they just grow wider.'"

"Don't worry, Dad," Morgan said. "You're in great shape."

"I hope you're right," Dad added. "We'll all have to be fit in order to hike up Half Dome."

They continued walking through the lower grove, passing by several more giant sequoias.

"There's the Clothespin Tree," Dad announced.

Mom looked at the tree. "That split in the trunk does make it look like an old-fashioned clothespin."

Farther down the trail were two trees growing together called the Faithful Couple. Mom smiled when she saw them. "Those trees look like you and me, Bob—always together."

Morgan bent down and picked up a cone. It was about the size of her big toe. She looked up at the tree. "This cone is so small for such a large tree," she commented.

"Its seeds are even smaller than that," Mom said. She opened up a cone and shook out a few of its seeds. They fell into her hand.

"They look like tiny oat flakes," James said.

RECIPE FOR A GIANT TREE

A mature giant sequoia tree may produce thousands of cones. Each cone contains about 200 seeds. Sequoia seeds are one-fourth of an inch long.

Sequoias need fires to reproduce. Fires clear space in the forest by killing off other types of plants and trees. This gives young sequoias the sunlight and soil they need to grow. A fire's heat also dries up green sequoia cones high in the tree. This causes the cones to drop fresh seeds onto the forest floor after a fire. A winter of snowfall combined with sunlight, moisture, fresh seeds, ash from the fire, and minerals in the soil make for perfect growing conditions to germinate sequoias.

Mom shook the seeds off her hand and into the dirt. She put the cone back on the ground. "Now that we have preserved groves like this, some of those seeds have a chance of becoming the largest living things on Earth."

"There sure are a lot of cones," James said while looking at a pile beneath the Bachelor Tree.

The family walked back toward the parking lot. On the way, they passed a tree that had fallen down. "The Fallen Monarch," James commented while looking at the trail guide.

The family inspected the large roots of the tree.

"They weren't very deep," Mom realized.

There were small sequoias nearby. "It looks like another generation of sequoias is already growing," Dad said.

"Good," Morgan added. "Years from now, I'll come back and check to see how they're doing."

The family got back in their car and Mom drove them back toward Upper Pines Campground in Yosemite Valley.

Along the way, they passed through a long tunnel. Once they were through the tunnel, there was a turnoff and a viewing area. Dozens of cars and a few tour buses were parked there. "Let me pull over," Mom said.

Mom parked the car and the Parkers piled out. They walked up to a railing with signs giving information. They gazed out at a perfect view of Yosemite Valley.

"Wow!" Dad exclaimed. "You can really see from here how glaciers helped shaped this place."

"Why do you say that?" Morgan asked.

"Mostly it's the U-shaped valley. But, also, Bridalveil Falls over there is coming from a hanging valley above the main valley floor. That's a sure sign that glaciers helped to carve parts of this area."

The family stood at the overlook for a few more minutes. Morgan snapped a picture of the family with the whole valley in the background.

"What do you say we head to camp now?" Mom suggested.

"I am hungry," James admitted.

...

After dinner at the campfire, James asked, "Can I borrow the car keys?"

"What for?" Mom replied.

"You'll see," James answered. He took the keys from Mom, walked over to the car, and opened the door.

Morgan looked up from her journal. "I wonder what he's doing." She turned to look at the campfire for a moment and then wrote.

> Dear Diary,
>
> It's our second night at the Upper Pines Campground in Yosemite Valley. And I love it here!
>
> Yesterday, James and I climbed eight pitches of rock with the help of our guide, Mike. I've never climbed more then one pitch before! In the end, we were 800 feet above the valley floor. It was an amazing view up there. I think I would like to rock climb some more now. I know James and I have been to climbing camp several times at an indoor gym, but I wonder what it would be like to climb other rocks in Yosemite. Maybe Mom and Dad can go with us next time. Or better yet, we can get the equipment and learn to set up the ropes and protection ourselves!
>
> I can't take my mind off the mother bear and cub I saw last night. Were they hurt when they were shot?
>
> Anyway, even though we've done so much, there's a lot more ahead for us here in Yosemite. So I'll write again as soon as I can.
>
> Until next time!
>
> Morgan

...

James shut the car door.

Mom, Dad, and Morgan looked up.

James walked over to the campfire, holding something in his hand. "Remember that warning sign outside our campground about the bears?"

"'This could happen to your vehicle,'" Morgan said.

"That's right," James said. "And 'A fed bear is a dead bear.' Also, 'Leaving food out of the bear lockers can be a $250 fine.' Just ask our neighbors." He held up two energy bars.

"I forgot I had put these in the jacket behind the seats. The car is all food-free now."

James walked over to the bear locker and put the energy bars inside.

James sat down by the campfire and wrote.

This is James Parker reporting.

Yosemite is amazing! The rock walls here are thousands of feet high. And rock climbers from all over the world are here to climb them. That's exactly what Morgan and I did yesterday. We climbed Ranger Rock, but it wasn't easy. I got stuck near the top, and I thought I was going to have to get rescued. But, luckily, Mike helped me get up the final pitch. Whew! That was a relief!

We saw an actor, Lee Stetson, play John Muir at the Yosemite Theater. It was cool to hear his stories. I especially liked the ones about his dog Stickeen. The actor said Muir thought no other mortal creature had taught him so much. Well, one day they were exploring a glacier. Muir crossed an ice bridge, but Stickeen wouldn't go. Stickeen got scared of the huge crevasse, but he was also afraid of getting left behind. Finally, after calling to him many times, Muir got Stickeen to cross the ice bridge. The dog ran right up to Muir and yelped and barked and danced around. After that, Muir said that Stickeen never left his side. It was a great story, but he also had many others, like the time he said he interviewed a bear. Morgan and I bought the book "Stickeen" to find out more about Muir and his dog on their other adventures.

I'll write more after our next great adventure here. I promise.

James

"There's Half Dome," James said.

The family gazed at the massive rock rising high above the other end of the valley.

"I wonder where Mark and Mike are on it now," Morgan said.

"I can't believe we're going to hike to the top of it," James added.

Mom laughed. "It's a good thing, then, that we're doing this *easy* trail now."

The family was hiking to the top of Yosemite Falls. They'd stopped at Columbia Rock to rest and gaze out over the valley.

Morgan pulled out her camera and took some pictures. She noticed a wooden building across the valley. "There's the chapel," she pointed out. "Can I use the binoculars?" she asked Mom.

Morgan focused in on the chapel. "I think there's a wedding going on!"

"A wedding?" Mom asked.

Morgan handed Mom the binoculars.

"Yep. A wedding," Mom agreed. "It looks like a great place for one too."

Farther up the trail, they came to a tiny stream. Dad sloshed his hat in the water and put it back on his head. Water dripped down his face. "Now that feels good!" he exclaimed. James and Morgan copied Dad.

They hiked on. Soon, all of upper Yosemite Falls came into view.

The water crashed onto the rocks below it.

"Yosemite Falls is the tallest waterfall in the United States," Dad said.

"In North America," James corrected Dad.

•••

In another part of the park, Mark, Mike, and a crew of people rode horses toward Half Dome.

They climbed a set of switchbacks and approached a small side trail. "That's the path we're taking from here on," Mike said to Mark. "But it's real steep. We'll have to get off the horses and hike the rest of the way."

Mark slid off his horse and onto Mike's back. He wrapped his arms around Mike's neck.

"Hold tight," Mike said.

A person from the crew tied a rope from Mark to Mike to secure his hold.

"How are you feeling?" Mike asked Mark.

"Great," Mark replied. "Just getting out into the backcountry has been a treat. You know, I haven't been able to come here since the accident. But I'm ready for the climb, if that's what you mean."

They walked off the main trail and onto the side trail. It was rocky, with a steep drop-off.

"I'm going to take my time here and watch my step," Mike said.

Mark looked down. "Please do. I'd hate to have us take a tumble here."

"To the base of Half Dome we go!" Mike announced.

...

The family looked up to the top of Yosemite Falls.

A narrow sliver of water plunged down from a gap at the top of the cliff. Then the waterfall opened up into a wide channel. Drifts of mist blew out from the falls and spread onto the cliffs and trees along the trail.

They hiked into a part of the trail surrounded by trees, mosses, and ferns. Wisps of mist drifted over them. A gentle cascade of water trickled down a nearby cliff.

"It's so nice and cool in here," Dad said.

"It's like we're entering a cloud forest," Mom added. "This area is its own little microclimate."

Soon they climbed out of the misty section and onto a drier part of the trail. They entered a steep canyon. The trail wove back and forth toward the top.

Morgan led the way, with James following her. Mom and Dad trailed behind. They could hear Yosemite Falls's pounding roar on the rocks below.

Morgan stopped for a moment. She gazed up at the massive cliff above her. James joined her.

"I wonder if any of those rocks ever come crashing down," James said.

"I hope not," Morgan replied.

Mom and Dad caught up. Dad wiped the sweat off his forehead and chugged down some water. "Need some, anyone?"

Mom, James, and Morgan each drank. They continued climbing up the switchbacks. Soon they were out of view of the falls. The trail continued to climb, but it was a bit more gradual. Scattered trees and scrub brush lined the trail, providing brief moments of shade while they walked.

Morgan and James walked over to a small stream. They dipped their hats in the water and placed them back on their heads. The cool, fresh water trickled down their faces.

Morgan pulled out her water bottle and took a long drink. A moment later, Mom and Dad caught up again.

"Climbing!" James replied in a commanding voice.

"Climb on!" Morgan called out officially.

. . .

Meanwhile, Mike carried Mark along a steep, rocky slope. The crew following them brought their climbing gear, equipment, food, and more than a week's worth of supplies.

They approached the bottom of Half Dome.

Mark looked up at the sheer cliff he was going to live on for the next week or longer. "That's one steep rock," he observed. He felt for the small box in his pocket. *It's still there,* he thought.

. . .

Soon the trail leveled off. Morgan, James, Mom, and Dad entered the forest. They quickly came to a junction.

Dad looked at the sign. "Which way should we go?"

"We want to go back-packing now!" James suggested jokingly.

Mom smiled. "I wish. But we would need our tent and sleeping bags."

"And bear canisters," Morgan added.

"I think we should head this way then," James announced. "To the top of the falls."

Morgan, Mom, and Dad followed James. He walked past granite boulders and tall pine trees.

"What kind of trees are those?" Morgan asked.

"Jeffrey pines, I believe," Mom replied. "I'm glad you're interested in the trees of the park."

The trail dipped down some rock steps. Gusts of wind blew up from the valley below.

James stopped. To the left of the trail were pools and cascades of tumbling, turbulent water in Yosemite Creek above the falls. "Boy, that's running fast," James remarked.

The trail veered to the right. A metal railing was embedded into the rock. James gripped it and slowly proceeded down some rock steps.

Dad caught up to James. "Careful here," he warned.

James stepped down to a flatter area of rock. "We made it!" he announced. At the edge of the rock was a railing protecting hikers from a long fall into the valley. James, Morgan, Mom, and Dad walked over to the railing. They gazed out at the view. Below them was Yosemite Valley with its meadows and the Merced River meandering through it.

To their left was the thundering plunge of Yosemite Falls.

HEAVY SNOW FALLS

The best time of year to see Yosemite's famous waterfalls is in spring or early summer. This is when snow is melting rapidly in the high mountains. The runoff feeds the waterfalls, which often flow in full force through April, May, and sometimes June. The waterfalls are almost dried up by late summer and sometimes stop running completely. In some years, Yosemite Falls is bone dry during August and September.

The family looked down.

"That is one long drop," Mom said.

Morgan, James, Mom, and Dad stood mesmerized by the view.

"I can sure see why John Muir wanted this place preserved," Dad commented.

"Pictures!" Morgan called out. "I almost forgot." She snapped several photos of the view and then a picture of her family standing at the railing.

Morgan put away her camera. "I wonder if we can see this spot from the valley," she said.

James looked up at Half Dome again.

Dad saw where James was looking. "If you think this trail was tough, wait until we do that one," Dad said.

The family looked at the view for a few more minutes. Then they gathered up their belongings and headed up the rock stairs to the trail and back down to the valley.

"Can I see?" James asked.

Mom handed James the binoculars.

Morgan, James, Mom, and Dad were having a picnic lunch next to a meadow in Yosemite Valley. They were watching the rock climbers on El Capitan.

Morgan pointed at the massive rock. "They're about halfway up, just above that part of the rock that looks like a heart."

James looked for a minute. "I see them!" he called out. "There are three climbers. It looks like they're hauling bags too."

"That must be their overnight gear," Dad explained. "You have to carry all that when you are scaling the single largest piece of granite in the world. That rock can take over a week to climb."

"What do they sleep on?" Morgan asked.

"Cots that they anchor into the rock," Mom answered.

"I don't think I would want to do that," James said. He handed the binoculars to Morgan.

"I'm not so sure I'd want you to do that either," Dad added. "But I would like all of us to go climbing together, maybe next time we come here."

"Honey," Mom said to Dad, "remember that time we came into Yosemite Valley at five in the morning?"

"That's right," Dad recalled. "It was totally dark, and we saw little dots of light on El Capitan. They were like tiny stars."

"They were the headlamps or cookstoves of climbers," Mom explained, then turned to Morgan. "Did you take pictures out here?" she asked. "I just love the meadows with the cliffs in the background. It's one of my favorite places in the valley."

"Good idea!" Morgan replied. She started looking around and snapping some photos.

After a while, the family packed up their picnic to do some sight-seeing in the valley.

While walking back to the car, James called out, "We're finally going backpacking tomorrow!"

Mom smiled. "Yes, finally."

The family drove to Yosemite Village to get supplies for their trip. They bought food at the market and stopped at the backcountry office to get wilderness camping permits and four bear canisters to store their food in while backpacking.

Afterwards, the family drove over to their camp-ground and put their food in the bear locker.

Once the food was put away, Morgan looked at her watch. "It's only five o'clock," she said. "Can we go to Mirror Lake?"

"It's only a short walk," James added.

"No need to explain further," Mom said. "Dad and I want to go too."

They walked over to the nearest bus stop.

"It's so nice that these buses are free," Dad said.

Morgan, James, Mom, and Dad got off the bus at the Mirror Lake stop. They walked up the paved road to the lake. Once they were there, James looked up. "There's Half Dome again," he announced.

Dad looked up at the giant sliced-in-half rock. "There's nothing like it anywhere in the world. And this time we get a close-up view."

"I wonder where Mark and Mike are now," James said. He stared at the huge rock for a moment. "I think I see someone!" James pulled the binoculars out of his pack and searched.

James focused on two climbers near the bottom of the gigantic dome.

"Can I see?" Morgan asked.

"Whoever it is, it looks like they just got started," James said. He handed the binoculars to Morgan.

Morgan looked through the binoculars. "I found them."

Morgan, James, Mom, and Dad watched the two climbers. "It doesn't seem like they're moving," Dad said.

"Maybe they're making dinner," Mom suggested.

"That can't be easy to do while hanging from ropes on a cliff," Dad said.

The family walked along Mirror Lake, a small lake with large boulders scattered around it.

Dad looked up at Half Dome rising far above the lake. "I bet these rocks came down from there," he said. "From what I understand," Dad added, "Mirror Lake is getting filled in each year by sediment coming down the canyon. It won't be a lake much longer."

"I'm glad we got to see it now, then," Mom said. "It is so peaceful out here."

Morgan and James walked up to the lake's calm waters. James picked up a rock and flung it into the lake.

Morgan threw one farther.

James turned and looked into the forest. "Did you hear that?"

Morgan spun around. "What?"

The family gazed into the woods surrounding Mirror Lake. The sun had long since dropped behind one of Yosemite's massive cliffs, which made the area dark and shady. Something cracked on the ground. "Now I heard something too," Mom said.

"Do you think there could be a bear out there?" James asked nervously.

"I don't know if we want to wait and find out," Dad answered. "Should we get going now?"

"Okay," James and Morgan quickly agreed.

They walked down the road past the bus stop and continued on toward Upper Pines Campground.

Morgan and James looked back to see if any bears, or anything else, was following them.

They came upon another bear trap truck parked next to the road. "I guess there are bears around here," Morgan realized. "But I don't really want to look in there and find out if one is trapped."

"But removing problem bears and getting them away from people is a good thing," Mom said.

The family finished their walk back to camp. They could smell dinner being cooked all around them.

"Right on time!" Dad announced. "This mountain air makes me as hungry as a bear!"

Dad patted his belly. "Man, I'm stuffed."

Morgan smiled. "No more s'mores for you!"

"At least for another twenty minutes," Dad joked.

The family started cleaning up camp for the evening. A couple of rangers walked up.

"Good evening," one of the rangers greeted them. "We're checking the campsites to make sure all food and anything with an odor is being stored in the bear lockers."

"We just started to put things away," Mom said.

"Great," the ranger went on. "We've had some bears around. In fact, a mother and a cub have been seen recently in this campground."

"I saw two bears the other night," Morgan interjected. "Except the mother got shot at and ran off into the woods. She had a tag on her left ear."

"Yes, we know that bear," the ranger said. "And those are rubber bullets the rangers used."

"Do the bullets hurt them?" Morgan asked.

"Just enough to scare them away from people. Which is exactly what we want," the other ranger explained. "Anyway, the best way to protect the bears—and your food—is to use the bear lockers."

The two rangers walked over to the next campsite.

About 300 to 500 black bears live in Yosemite National Park. Even though they are called black bears, their color can range from cinnamon to brown to black. Male black bears can weigh up to 350 pounds. Black bears have a powerful sense of smell. They can easily seek out human food, which is really bad for them. It's best that they eat wild food. Black bears eat grasses, berries, acorns, and insects. During late summer and into fall, they can consume up to 20,000 calories of food per day!

Yosemite's bears live in meadows, in forests, or at higher elevations. They are most active at night but can be seen at any time of the day. Yosemite rangers are actively monitoring the park's bears. They try to tag all of them. Visitors should report all bear sightings.

• • •

Mark turned off his cookstove. He carefully shifted himself around on his port-a-ledge and peered down at the cliff below him. "Nothing like a bed with a view!" he exclaimed. Mark took some hot water and slowly poured it into his cup of powdered soup. He stirred the soup and took a sip. "Ahhh. A well-deserved meal now begins."

"Yep," Mike said. "We've climbed about 200 feet so far, but we worked hard for every inch of it."

Mark took a bite from a cookie and a long drink from his soup. He turned off his light and gazed out at the universe of stars above. Then he leaned his head back and looked straight up at the stark, towering silhouette of the top of Half Dome rising more than a thousand feet above him.

Multiday rock climbs take a lot of preparation and special gear. Climbers staying overnight on rock walls usually use port-a-ledges to sleep on. These cotlike devices attach to a rock and keep a climber reasonably comfortable while sleeping. Climbers also need extra rope and haul bags to carry their supplies. Food and water on long climbs can weigh more than all the other climbing gear. A week or more on Half Dome might mean 200 or more pounds of equipment to haul up the cliff!

. . .

While Mom and Dad read, James walked over to the picnic table and lay down. He grabbed his binoculars and examined some of the stars. Morgan joined James. "There's the Milky Way!" James pointed out.

"You see so many more stars here than at home," Morgan said.

Later that evening, James lay down in his tent. He turned the knob on his headlamp until the light shone on his journal. He picked up his pen and wrote.

This is James Parker reporting.

It's the last night that I will have my tent all to myself for a while. We are all going backpacking tomorrow, and Morgan and I are going to share a tent to cut down on the weight in our packs.

I can't wait to see the places I've been looking at on our map for so long. John Muir said that the Hetch Hetchy area is just as beautiful as Yosemite Valley. It looks like there will be a lot of steep climbs on the trail. But it's not like we haven't been climbing on our hikes already.

And when we're done with our backpack, we get to do the Grand Finale climb: Half Dome. Now that will be something worth writing about!

I know I'll have more to write soon.

Reporting from Yosemite,

James Parker

Morgan rolled over in her tent. "I can't sleep," she mumbled, sitting up. Morgan found her flashlight and turned it on. She unzipped her tent and shone her light all around. Nothing seemed to be moving. No people, no bears, and no rangers looking for bears. "I know we put all our cooking stuff away," she assured herself.

Morgan looked at Mom and Dad's tent and over at James's. All seemed still and quiet. "I think I'm the only person awake in all of Yosemite," she said to herself.

Morgan found her sandals and got dressed. She clambered out of her tent and saw the bathroom light a couple of campsites away. Morgan scampered there as fast as she could.

Morgan washed her hands and looked into the mirror. "I guess I won't see this face for a while. I wonder how dirty I'll be when we come back." Morgan dried her hands and walked out the door.

And froze.

Ten feet away from Morgan was a large black bear.

The bear stared at Morgan.

Morgan backed up a few feet, pressing her back against the bathroom door.

Morgan swallowed nervously. "It's okay, big bear," she managed to say.

There was a noise in the bushes. Morgan kept her light shining on the bear.

The bear looked toward the noise, then back at Morgan.

"Go on. Get out of here," Morgan squeaked.

The bear huffed out a breath of air and lumbered off into the woods.

Morgan shone her flashlight all around and then dashed toward her parents' tent. She hurried inside and snuggled up with Mom and Dad. "What's up?" Mom asked.

"You don't know?" Morgan replied. She told her parents about the bear in camp.

Morgan spent the rest of the night in her parents' tent.

. . .

The next morning, Morgan got her journal out of her tent and wrote.

Dear Diary,

Guess what? I saw a bear last night outside the camp bathroom! It stared at me for a long time before it finally ran away. I hardly slept last night because of it!

There's so much more to write about. But all I can think of is that bear. Is it the same bear I saw the other day? If it is, where is its cub? And what will happen to it if it keeps coming into this campground? Will they trap it and move it away? To where?

Anyway, our big backpack starts today. I hope we don't see any bears out there. I'll write about that trip soon.

Reporting the bear facts,

Morgan

Morgan, James, Mom, and Dad spent three days backpacking in the Hetch Hetchy area.

They camped at Laurel Lake and Lake Vernon the first two nights. Now, on their third night, they were camped at Rancheria Falls. It was the last night of their backpacking trip.

Several hundred yards below Rancheria Falls, Morgan knelt down next to a calm section of water and pumped the water filter. James held the hose inside the mouth of a bottle. Slowly, the bottle filled with clean, drinkable water.

James and Morgan finished pumping the water and carried everything over to camp.

Mom was slicing apples. She stopped and greeted Morgan and James. "Thanks for replenishing our water supply."

Dad looked up from stirring the chili over the tiny stove. "That's one of the things about backpacking that I love: cold, fresh water!" he commented. "Are you ready to eat?"

Dad dished out the chili. They each took a bowl and sat down on logs set up around the campfire ring.

James blew on his chili to cool it off.

A deer approached the area. "Look," Mom whispered.

The deer nibbled at some grass and then gazed at the family. It flicked its ears and trotted to a new spot and nibbled some more.

"We don't get to see something like that at home, that's for sure," Mom commented.

Thunder rumbled far away.

"I just got hit by a raindrop," James called out.

They all looked up. Dark clouds had gathered overhead. Distant thunder rumbled again. Scattered drops of rain plopped down, and the campfire hissed and steamed.

They each put on a windbreaker.

Dad studied the sky. "Hopefully, we'll be able to finish our dinner outside."

• • •

Rain poured down on top of the rain fly covering Mark's port-a-ledge.

Mark checked all the knots on his harness, his port-a-ledge, and in the rock to make sure they were secure. Then he slid deeper into his bag. Mark pulled the drawstring tight around his head so that only his nose and eyes were exposed. "It's going to be a long night," he concluded.

The sky lit up. Thunder instantly boomed all around him. It started raining even harder.

"It's not usually like this in Yosemite in June," Mike said. "At this rate, who knows when we'll get to the top."

One thousand feet above the base of Half Dome, and well over 3,000 feet above the valley floor, Mark's port-a-ledge rattled and swayed with the wind. The metal protection and anchors clanked against each other and the rock.

It started hailing. Drops of rain and hail smacked against the rock and rain fly. Mark closed his eyes and turned his face sideways. The rain and hail continued. Mark started shivering. He wondered when his next hot meal would be and whether they'd be able to even climb tomorrow.

Mark scrunched up his body into a tight ball and tried to stay warm. The tiny box in his pocket pressed into his hip.

• • •

Morgan and James joined Mom and Dad in their tent. They were bundled up in warm clothes. Mom's headlamp dangled from the ceiling of the tent, lighting up the inside. Dad discarded a ten of spades onto a pile of cards. Steady rain continued to drip down outside.

"I wonder how much it's raining in Yosemite Valley now," Dad said.

"I wonder what bears do in a storm like this," Morgan said.

"Probably what we're doing," Mom commented. "Trying to stay warm and dry."

James picked up a card from the top of the deck.

Lightning lit up the sky. James counted. "1, 2, 3, 4, 5, 6, 7, 8, 9, 10, 11, 12." Thunder boomed. "It's a couple of miles away," he said, discarding a three of diamonds.

"Three of diamonds?" Dad said while the rain came down a bit harder. "I thought you wanted that card." Thunder rumbled again.

James smiled. "Not anymore. Gin!" James showed all his cards.

"So, James wins again," Morgan said. "Well, just wait until tomorrow night!"

• • •

Later that night, Morgan and James were in their tent.

James sat and listened to the rain. He slid out of his sleeping bag

Wapama Falls

and grabbed his headlamp. James unzipped the tent, put on his shoes, and walked outside. "I'll be right back," he announced to Morgan.

Morgan turned onto her side and started writing.

Dear Diary,

It seems like every time I write to you, there's so much to tell. And the same is true now.

The first night of this backpack we camped at forested Laurel Lake, and we got to swim briefly in the water there. Then we hiked to Lake Vernon, which was surrounded by granite. After climbing out of there, we even passed by a few patches of snow. We finally made it to where we are now, Rancheria Falls, our last night of the three-day backpack. This is my favorite of the three campsites. The waterfall is so close, we can hear it roar from camp.

Tomorrow we hike back to our car and return to Yosemite Valley.

The day after tomorrow we head to the top of Half Dome! What a trip!

Trying to stay warm and dry,
Morgan

James shuffled back into the tent.

"How is it out there?" Morgan asked.

"Cold and wet," James answered. "I can see my breath. But it's hardly raining now. The stars are out."

"Did you see anything?" Morgan asked nervously.

"No bears, if that's what you mean," James replied. "But to be honest, I wasn't looking for any. I just wanted to go to the bathroom and get back in here as fast as possible."

"Well, Mom and Dad's tent is just a few feet away," Morgan said. "We should be okay."

James slithered into his sleeping bag. He noticed Morgan's journal lying next to her. "My turn to write," he announced. He pulled out his journal.

This is James Parker reporting.

It's our last night of our three-night journey near Hetch Hetchy Reservoir in Yosemite. I wish we were going farther. I can picture myself being like John Muir and hiking endlessly for days and nights and going for hundreds of miles. I know Muir did a thousand-mile walk once. But this trip has only been about twenty-three miles of hiking so far.

We saw a deer in camp tonight. It was fun watching it. I kind of hope we see a bear. But not if it is up close. At the John Muir show we saw the other day, the actor talked about John Muir interviewing a bear. Wouldn't that be fun? What would I ask it? Something like, do you like living in Yosemite? And are you getting enough natural food? What is your favorite food anyway? Don't you realize that people food is bad for you?

Mom and Dad have talked about coming back here one spring. I'd like to see what Yosemite's waterfalls look like in April when the snow is really melting. They're huge enough now. How much bigger can they be?

Anyway, reporting from Rancheria Falls Camp in Yosemite National Park, this is James Parker saying good night!

James Parker

"Are you guys ready?" James called out.

Morgan snapped several pictures of Wapama Falls with Hetch Hetchy Reservoir in the background and quickly put her camera back in the plastic bag. "Ready," Morgan answered. She followed James onto the wooden bridge.

James turned around and grinned at his family. "We're going to get soaked!"

The driving waterfall splashed over the bridge and tumbled and churned its way to the reservoir below.

They crept farther along and into the middle of the tumult. Water showered all around them. James stood and faced the waterfall while opening his arms wide. "Finally, a shower!" he joked.

Mom hurried across the bridge then turned back to look at James and Morgan.

"Okay, here goes," Dad called out. He ran across the bridge as fast as he could.

Once he was off the bridge, Dad turned around and looked back. "There are two rainbows," he said, "right over the reservoir."

"Now I have to get a picture of that!" Morgan exclaimed.

Soon they left the thundering waterfall behind and were hiking in dry country again.

• • •

"That was one scary night!" Mike exclaimed while hauling up a gear bag.

Mark looked up. "I don't think I slept much. The wind knocked me against the rock all night long."

"I was sure surprised to wake up to an inch of snow on top of my sleeping bag!" Mike added.

"Well, it's all melted now," Mark said. He pulled himself up once more and put his hand on the rock face. "The rock is so cold. Let's stop and get something warm to eat, okay?"

• • •

"I wonder what this whole valley would look like if the dam wasn't there," Morgan said.

James took a bite out of some jerky. He chewed it slowly while looking up at another waterfall and out at the reservoir.

Mom looked out. "I believe that several Native American archaeological sites are buried under the water."

James, Morgan, Mom, and Dad sat in the shade on some rocks near the trail. "I wish we could see them," James said.

Morgan gazed at the long blue reservoir. Across the water, Kolana Rock jutted upward more than a thousand feet.

"This was the perfect environment for Native Americans," Dad said. "There was plenty of game, great soil for crops, oak trees with acorns, and lots of water.

"John Muir wanted to protect Hetch Hetchy Valley," Dad went on. "He thought it was Yosemite Valley's twin and just as beautiful. But instead, people built a dam here."

"Hmm," James said. He tried to imagine what the valley would look like if a river ran through it and there were trails and campgrounds at the bottom.

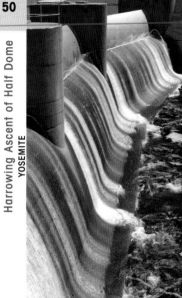

John Muir helped save Yosemite Valley, but despite a fierce battle, he wasn't able to preserve Yosemite's other famous valley, Hetch Hetchy. Muir first visited Hetch Hetchy Valley in 1871. It has towering granite cliffs and spectacular waterfalls, similar to Yosemite Valley. In the early 1900s, Hetch Hetchy Valley became part of a long political battle over water. Eventually, Congress passed the Raker Act in 1913, which allowed for Hetch Hetchy Valley to be flooded. John Muir died in 1914. Meanwhile, Hetch Hetchy's dam was completed in 1923. Since then, the lower part of Hetch Hetchy Valley has been underwater. The water stored there is used by the city of San Francisco. Muir was distraught over losing Hetch Hetchy Valley to a reservoir. Some people still feel the way Muir did. Conservation groups are currently studying new areas that can be used for water storage so Hetch Hetchy can become a wild valley again.

The family ate for a few more minutes.

Dad stood up and put on his backpack. "Ready, everyone?"

James, Morgan, Mom, and Dad headed westward on the trail skirting Hetch Hetchy.

"I can't believe how light my pack feels now," James said.

"I can't believe how dirty you look!" Morgan called out.

"Hey, you're not exactly Mr. Clean!" James retorted.

They came to a tunnel carved through the mountain.

"Exit the wilderness!" James announced.

The family tramped through the tunnel. They walked to the middle of Hetch Hetchy Dam. Water poured from the dam and into the

Tuolumne River below it.

"The drinking fountain is still on!" Morgan called out. She ran over and got a long, cool drink. "It's weird to have a drinking fountain out here in the middle of a dam."

"I guess they just leave this thing running all the time," Mom said.

The family stood near the drinking fountain and gazed out at Hetch Hetchy. Wapama Falls looked so small in the distance. A little closer to the dam, Tueelalala Falls looked like a soft, thin sliver of water cascading down.

"How about one more picture?" Morgan asked.

Morgan lined her family up to get a photo of them with their packs on. Behind them was Hetch Hetchy and the surrounding area where they had just backpacked. She snapped the photo.

The family trudged up the road to their car in the overnight parking lot.

Buzzzzz!

Click.

James shut off the alarm clock. "It's time, everyone!"

Dad yawned. "It is?"

"It's 5:30," James answered. "See!" He held the clock face toward his father.

"Well, at least we got a soft bed, warm showers, and a good night's sleep, right?" Mom said.

"Right," Morgan answered. "One night in Yosemite Lodge was worth it."

"Come on," Mom urged. "Now that we're up early, let's take advantage of it and get going."

"This could be the hardest hike we'll ever do," Dad said while stuffing four large garbage bags into his backpack.

After packing, Mom, Dad, James, and Morgan drove to Curry Village and parked.

. . .

Mark yawned and stretched. "How far do you think we have to go?"

"Hopefully we'll make it to the top today," Mike answered. He took a long gulp of water.

Mark started taking apart his port-a-ledge and setting up his rope.

Mike looked into the food bag. "There's not much left." He reached all the way to the bottom. "Do you mind sharing?" He held up a bag of dried fruit.

"That's all?" Mark asked.

A deafening crack ripped through the air.

Mark instinctively looked up.

Another crack boomed even louder. Mark saw a slab of granite peeling off Half Dome. It looked like it was moving in slow motion.

The rock fell outward. It started tumbling down the cliff and breaking apart.

"Rockfall!" Mark shouted.

Mark watched the jumbled mass of rocks and boulders shower down. He put his hands over his head and ducked.

The rock cascade pounded on Mark and Mike and pinballed its way down the cliff. A cloud of dust filled the air. Mark kept himself protected as the debris pummeled down.

. . .

A booming roar echoed across the valley. The thundering sound rolled on for several seconds.

Morgan, James, Mom, and Dad stood still.

"What is that?" James said.

The rumbling continued then slowly faded.

"It sounds like there was a rockfall," Dad said.

Morgan looked around. "Everything seems the same to me."

A large group of hikers whisked by, heading up.

Mom looked at the hikers then up at the cliffs. "We'd better get going."

The family trudged up the first part of the trail. They hiked on silently, enjoying the cool morning and the sound of the rushing water from the Merced River next to the trail.

. . .

Mark slowly peeked out from under his arms. The rockfall had passed. He coughed several times and shook off some of the rock dust. He looked below. A few loose rocks trickled down the steep hill below the dome.

Mark looked up. No more rocks were falling. He checked himself for cuts and bruises but didn't find anything.

Then he heard Mike moan in pain. He was hanging from his rope, slumped over, holding his arm.

. . .

James pointed to a side canyon. "I wonder if the rockfall was up there."

The family glanced at a long, steep area full of large rocks and boulders.

"Well, if the rocks came down from there, we should be okay," Dad concluded. "It's pretty far away."

James looked at the top of the side canyon. "Hey, there's another waterfall up there!"

"They're all over the place in this park," Mom commented.

They walked briskly uphill, keeping pace with the other early morning hikers.

"It's like being on a conveyor belt," Dad said. "Everyone is walking so fast."

Morgan caught up to Mom. "We all have one goal in mind: to get to the top of Half Dome."

"And to see the scenery and waterfalls along the way," Mom added.

A while later, they came to a footbridge and stopped in the middle of it. In the distance was a huge curtain of water cascading straight down.

"That must be Vernal Falls!" James gasped.

Morgan snapped a few pictures.

Morgan, James, Mom, and Dad hiked on.

. . .

Mark looked up at Mike. "Are you all right?"

Mike grimaced while holding his arm. "I don't know," he replied. "Give me a moment."

Mark dangled from his rope. He rechecked himself to see if he had any cuts or bruises. "I'm lucky," he realized.

Mike pulled himself toward a rock ledge. He grabbed on with one arm and managed to stand up.

Mark watched as Mike gingerly rolled up his sleeve. There was a deep gash on his arm. It was oozing blood. Mike shut his eyes and leaned up against the cliff.

. . .

"Here we go!" Dad called out. He led his family up a series of rock stairs. The higher Dad climbed, the wetter the stairs became. The crashing sound of Vernal Falls grew louder with each step.

Dad turned around and grinned at his family. "I love this!" he called out.

The trail got soggier. Mom looked up at the veils of mist above them. She watched several hikers climb quickly through the spray and saw how soaked they got. "I think it's time for those garbage bags, honey."

Dad handed out the four garbage bags. Mom, Dad, Morgan, and

James each punctured a hole at the top of their bag and pulled on it to make it larger. They slipped the bags over their heads and draped them over their upper body and packs.

"Ready?" Dad shouted over the roar of the falls.

"Ready!" Morgan, James, and Mom answered.

They took off uphill and were quickly sprayed by gusts of wind and water.

"It's like we're in the middle of a raging storm at sea," Morgan said.

"Keep walking," Mom urged them.

Morgan, James, Mom, and Dad hurried up the wet, rocky stairs. To the left of them, Vernal Falls thundered down.

Dad carefully surged ahead while stepping into deep puddles of water. He came to a large rock that protected his family from the onslaught. They gathered together behind the rock.

"How are you?" Mom asked Morgan.

"Just cold and wet," Morgan answered through chattering teeth.

Dad looked at the trail. "We're not out of the shower yet."

Morgan, James, Mom, and Dad plowed on. The mist got heavier, but then quickly let up. A short while later, James turned around with a big smile on his face. "We made it!"

They looked down at the other hikers getting soaked.

"Boy, that was something," Dad said.

They each took off their garbage bag, shook it off, then stuffed it into their pack.

The trail climbed up more steep stairs. They came to a spot with some rails and hiked up the jagged, rocky steps along them. A moment later, they walked down a granite slope. They were at the top of Vernal Falls, looking down.

The Parkers walked right to the railing.

A rushing curtain of water disappeared over the cliff in front of them.

Mom looked down at the crashing water below. "The view of a lifetime!" she exclaimed.

They stood at the brink of the falls a moment longer.

"Better keep moving," Mom suggested. "We can always take our time on the way back down."

They walked upstream a short distance.

Dad pointed to a raging, turbulent pool of water. "Look at that!" Large chunks of wood whisked around in the current. A racing cascade plunged into the pool like a gigantic waterslide.

"I think that's Emerald Pool," James said.

"It's so powerful," Dad observed. "There must be a lot of snow melting in the mountains above here."

They continued hiking and came to a small footbridge.

"Look up there!" James exclaimed.

The family got their first glimpse of an even taller waterfall. Morgan started taking pictures. "Is that Nevada Falls?"

"Yep," Dad responded. "And that huge round-shaped rock is Liberty Cap."

"Do you think it was formed by glaciers?" James asked.

"Good question, James." Dad replied. "The polished-looking rock on those domes is a sign that glaciers were part of Yosemite's geologic past. We've also passed some glacial polish along the trail. Glaciers ran over the rock, which was made smooth and worn over the years by the weight of the ice."

• • •

Mark looked up at Mike. "How bad is your arm?"

Mike grimaced. "I don't know," Mike replied. Using mostly his uninjured arm, Mike worked with his anchors to secure himself.

Mark climbed up his rope, maneuvered over to Mike, and anchored himself in. He reached into a gear bag and grabbed the first-aid kit.

Mark dabbed Mike's cut and cleaned his arm, but it kept bleeding. "A rock must have glanced right off of it," Mike complained.

Mark pulled out gauze. Together they finished cleaning and wrapping Mike's arm.

Mike took a deep breath. "I don't want to be rescued. We've planned this climb for far too long."

• • •

Morgan and James led the way up another series of rock stairs. The path was steep and smoothly worn by previous hikers. To their right, Nevada Falls thundered down onto a pile of rocks below.

Morgan and James kept a brisk pace. Mom and Dad were a few steps behind. The constant roar of the waterfall faded away as they moved farther up the trail. Soon, the waterfall was out of sight.

Morgan, James, Mom, and Dad hiked up more switchbacks. They came to a junction. One way headed toward Half Dome. The other way went to the top of Nevada Falls then back down to the valley.

The family rested for a few minutes, drank some water, and ate some snacks.

"I believe we're at the junction of the John Muir Trail," Dad said.

Shortly beyond the junction, the trail leveled out. To the right of the trail, the Merced River meandered along a forested valley.

"I bet we're in Little Yosemite Valley," Mom announced. "Dad and I talked about backpacking up to here. That way we would have had a shorter day hike to the top of Half Dome. But then we thought it would be better if we didn't have to haul our backpacks so far."

"I think that was a good decision," Dad huffed. "Those stairs were steep."

A junction in the trail led to Little Yosemite Valley's information station, backcountry campsites, and compost toilet.

The family took the short side trail to the backpacker area. They took off their packs and took turns climbing the wooden stairs to the bathroom. While waiting, Morgan read the information board.

"There's something here about bears," Morgan announced.

"Really?" Mom asked. She and Dad came over to look.

The bulletin board had several pictures of bears on it.

A ranger walked up. "Yep, those are the famous bears of Little Yosemite Valley."

Mom turned toward the ranger. "There are quite a few."

Morgan pointed to one of the pictures. "That one looks like the one I saw in our campground."

"I wonder if a bear would travel that far," Dad said.

"They certainly can travel that far," the ranger commented.

James climbed down the stairs and joined his family.

Morgan, James, Mom, and Dad slipped their daypacks back on.

They returned to the John Muir Trail heading toward Half Dome.

A few minutes later, Mom looked up and pointed. "There it is!"

The family abruptly stopped and gazed at a massive, double-humped bulge of rock.

Dad gasped. "I think we're looking at the rounded side of Half Dome!"

"You mean we're going up that?" Morgan asked.

"To the top," Mom said with an adventurous smile.

PEELING DOMES

Yosemite's natural landmarks include spectacular dome-shaped rocks. Half Dome is the most famous of these features. North Dome, Lembert, Pothole, and Wawona are other well-known domes in Yosemite.

These domes are created by a process called exfoliation. Granite slabs on the domes weather or peel off in layers rather than by grains. This can happen in very thin layers of rock or in thick slabs. Plant roots and freezing water getting into cracks often causes this to occur as well.

Mark's cell phone rang. "Hello. ... People heard the rockfall all the way from the valley? ... Yes, Mike is hurt, we aren't sure how badly. But at least we've stopped the bleeding. ... Well, you know Mike," Mark explained. "He doesn't want help. I'm not sure if we'll make it, but we're going to try. ... I'm okay," Mark said. "This climb means a lot to us, you know that. One way or another, I'm determined to get to the top. Hopefully, it won't be long now. But, yes, have the medic ready and waiting."

Mark said good-bye and hung up the phone.

"My lungs are burning," Dad complained.

"We're almost there. Look at how close the dome is," Morgan urged Dad on.

"How's everyone's water?" Mom asked.

"I've got a bottle and a half," James answered.

Morgan, James, Mom, and Dad trudged on. They were beyond Little Yosemite Valley now and gradually but steadily climbing. Parts of the trail passed through dense stands of forest, and other areas were more open and rocky.

Suddenly Morgan stopped. "Look!" She got out the binoculars.

Morgan focused the binoculars on Half Dome. "Yep, there are people up there," she said.

"Where?" James asked.

Morgan handed the binoculars to James. "On that stretch of rock."

"They're on the cables!" James realized.

James watched for a moment and then handed the binoculars to Mom. "I can't believe we're going to be climbing that," he said.

The family hiked on. They came to a junction and took the path that read "Half Dome: Two Miles." James looked at the sign. "That means we've gone about six and a half miles so far."

"We've come a long way," Mom encouraged. "We're getting there!"

Along a steep set of switchbacks they got their first good look at the

sheer cliff side of Half Dome. A faint trail branched off the main trail toward the base of the dome.

"I wonder what that trail is for," Dad said to Morgan.

The Parkers hiked on.

Dad pointed toward the valley. "There are Royal Arches and North Dome." Then he turned around. "And I think that's Cloud's Rest behind us."

"Where's Mom and Dad's Rest?" Mom joked.

The trail leveled off. They walked across the flatter area and passed a group of tents set up next to some horses.

Morgan, James, Mom, and Dad stopped to take a break in the shade beneath some tall pines.

"This may be our last chance to get out of the sun for a while," Dad said. He looked up at the hikers heading up some rocky switchbacks. "Boy, that looks steep."

. . .

Mike looked at the tightly wrapped gauze covering his arm. The blood was soaking through. He reached up to place a piece of protection in the rock. "Ahh!" Mike winced. But he managed to tap the gear into the rock and get the rope in it. "Let me check to make sure it will hold first," he said to Mark.

Mark hung on his rope and watched Mike work with the gear. His stomach growled. "Food," he grumbled. "We need food."

"It seems like I've been hungry since the first day up here," Mike called down. "The rope is secure now. You can resume climbing."

. . .

James finished his energy bar. He stood up and hoisted his pack back on.

"Ready now?" Dad asked James.

"Ready," James answered.

Morgan, James, Mom, and Dad followed other hikers up a series of windy, rocky stairs cut into the granite. The steps were steep and exposed. "I feel like we're climbing into heaven," Morgan said.

"Maybe we are," James said.

A gust of wind blew against them. Morgan grabbed onto her hat and held it on her head.

Dad looked out at the scenery. "Just climbing to see this view was worth it."

. . .

A small crowd of onlookers was now gathered on top of Half Dome watching Mike and Mark.

"I've got extra energy bars!" someone shouted down.

Mark and Mike both looked up. "Thanks, but no thanks," Mark replied. Then he looked at Mike. "Do we have any food left?"

"One granola bar. That's it," Mike said.

"You sure you don't want anything?" the person asked again.

"Nope," Mark answered. "We made a deal with each other that we wouldn't accept any help, no matter how long it takes."

"What is this now, our seventh day?" Mark asked Mike.

"Who's counting?" Mike replied.

"Seven days of living on rock," Mark reflected. His stomach growled while he anchored himself next to Mike. Once he made sure he was secure, Mark started pulling in the excess rope behind him. Mark coiled the rope as best he could onto the tiny ledge where they were perched.

Mike started setting up his next anchor. "One final pitch," he said.

"How's your arm?" Mark asked.

Mike looked at Mark. "I'm trying not to think about it. But since you asked, yes, it hurts."

. . .

James looked down and saw several hikers climbing the rock stairs. "I'm glad we're not down there," he said.

"We were a few minutes ago," Morgan reminded him.

Dad slowly took several more steps up the granite staircase. "Let's press on."

Soon the trail up the rock stairs leveled off. With renewed momentum, the family surged forward. Several steps later, they made it to the top of that part of the trail.

Morgan, James, Mom, and Dad stopped for a moment. Ahead of them was the final ascent up Half Dome. Straight up the dome were two cables about a sidewalk's width apart. Wooden planks were placed at intervals between the cables.

STEP RIGHT UP!

Josiah Whitney came to Yosemite in 1863 as part of a California Geological Survey. When he first saw Half Dome, he said it was "perfectly inaccessible." Twelve years later, George Anderson drilled holes and put in spikes for what is now the popular cable route. Anderson was the first person to climb Half Dome.

"We're going up that!" Morgan exclaimed. "It kind of looks like our climb up Ranger Rock, except much longer and without the gear."

James counted the wooden planks. "There are about forty-five."

The family watched several groups of hikers climb up Half Dome. One by one, the hikers slid their hands up the cables and pulled themselves along. Some of the climbers rested at each wooden plank before continuing their ascent.

"It's so long," James whispered.

"And so steep," Morgan added.

A couple of hikers walked past the family, heading back down.

"How was it?" Mom asked.

"We don't know," one of the hikers answered. "We chickened out and decided this was far enough for us."

Morgan looked at James.

James looked at his parents.

"We've come this far, we should at least give it a try," Mom said.

They walked toward the base of the dome. At the start of the cables was a sign. It warned "Beware. If a thunderstorm is anywhere on the horizon DO NOT PASS BEYOND THIS SIGN. Lightning has struck Half Dome during every month of the year."

James looked at the sky. "Just a few small clouds," he said.

"I hope they don't build up too quickly," Dad added.

"Hey, look at these!" Morgan called out.

Next to the sign was a pile of dozens of old, used, and tattered gloves.

Mom looked at people climbing and saw that everyone was wearing a pair. "They must help you grip the cables."

"Let's see if we each can find some that fit," Dad said.

. . .

Mike wrapped a piece of duct tape over some cuts along his thumb and palm. "I wonder how much good skin I have left," he muttered. Then he dipped his hand in his chalk bag.

Mike reached up as high as he could and wedged in one final piece of protection. He set his foot onto a tiny bulge in the rock. Then he hoisted himself up and slipped the rope into the protection piece. Mike climbed farther until the rope was taut. "I need some slack!" he called down to Mark.

Mark tried to feed out more rope. "That's all I've got!" Mark said. He looked behind him and pulled on the rope. "The rope is stuck!"

Oh, no! Mike thought. *What next?*

"Here we go," Mom said.

She grabbed one cable and started climbing until she made it to the first plank of wood. Mom stopped and turned around. "So far, so good," she said.

Mom continued to lead the way. Morgan and James followed her, with Dad in the back.

"It's like climbing a ladder," Morgan said as she joined Mom.

James and Dad were close behind.

Mom led the way farther up the cables. The rock surface was slick and worn down.

"It's like we're doing pull-ups," James said. "Just like Mark and his special bar, except our feet are also on the rock."

James looked down. His heart jumped. "Oops. Don't do what I just did."

"Looking down is scary, isn't it?" Dad agreed.

"I don't even want to think about what would happen if we lost our grip," Mom said.

. . .

Mark whipped the rope back and forth. It didn't budge. He pulled the rope toward him, but that only tightened it more.

"I can't get the rope loose!" he shouted.

Mike looked up. The crowd at the top had grown. A cameraman was filming them.

Mark tried to whip the rope loose again. "It's wedged between the rocks," he explained. Mark shifted his position as much as he could. He shook the rope several more times, but without success.

"I'm going to have to climb back down there," Mike said.

Mike looked down. He unclipped the rope from protection pieces and lowered himself to where Mark was.

. . .

Mom took a deep breath and climbed on.

"I wish I could take a picture," Morgan said. "But I'm afraid to take my hands off the cables."

Someone above them screamed. "I can't do this anymore!"

A woman was sitting on the rock and hugging one of the poles that held the cables in place. Tears were streaming down her face. The family moved up to her. "Can we help you?" Mom asked.

"It's okay, we're with her," a lady with a daypack said to Mom.

"This is too much!" the woman pleaded to her group. "Get me off of here now!"

Morgan, James, Mom, and Dad climbed past the woman. The family regathered at the wooden plank above the frightened climber.

"I hope she gets

down okay," Mom said.

"Are you all right?" Dad asked the twins with concern.

"I am," James replied.

"Me too," Morgan agreed.

Mom looked down. "There's a group coming up behind us," she said. "We'd better keep moving." Mom resumed climbing. But now, there were several people coming down the cables.

The people going down approached Mom. One by one, Morgan, James, Mom, and Dad put both their hands on one cable so the people going down could grab onto the other one.

"Is it easier going down?" Morgan asked a person going by.

The climber looked at Morgan. "In some ways," she replied. "As long as I don't look straight down!"

"Is the view worth it?" Dad asked the last person in the group.

"Oh, absolutely," he answered. "There's even a large patch of snow up there. And there's some sort of climbing rescue going on."

Mom surged on, pulling herself up the cables. Her family followed. The rock angle eased a bit, and they no longer continued resting at each plank. Momentum pulled them forward. They were approaching the top.

The angle of the rock lessened again.

Morgan caught up with Mom. "We're almost there!" she called out.

The family climbed some more. Finally, the rock flattened out and the cables ended.

"We made it!" James exclaimed.

Morgan, James, Mom, and Dad gathered together and strode forward onto Half Dome.

"That was one scary climb!" Dad said.

The top of the dome was all granite, scattered with rocks and boulders. It was easy to walk on.

"I can't believe how much room there is up here," Mom said.

"It feels like we're walking on the moon," Morgan added.

"There's the snowfield," James called out. The family looked at a large patch of dirty snow. Water trickled away from it. Two people were chasing each other and throwing snowballs.

"A snow fight in June," Dad said. "Who would have thought?"

"Hey, look!" James called out.

A large crowd was gathered at the edge of the dome. The people were looking down, watching something.

"I wonder if that has to do with Mark and Mike," Morgan said.

"Let's go over there and find out," Mom suggested.

Morgan, James, Mom, and Dad walked up to the crowd.

Morgan got out her camera. She walked close to the edge of Half Dome and looked down.

"Don't get too close," Dad warned.

Morgan peeked over the edge of the dome. "It *is* Mike and Mark!"

Mark belayed Mike until he was able to reach the stuck rope. He yanked at the rope, but it didn't budge.

"You can do it!" Morgan yelled.

Mike looked up and shielded his eyes from the sun. The voice sounded familiar. He moved closer to the rope and pulled it in a different direction. It popped loose.

The crowd cheered.

James recognized Mark's girlfriend in the crowd. "Hey, Kimberly!"

Kimberly smiled. "Hi there."

"Have you been waiting up here long?" Morgan asked.

"I arrived shortly before you. We've been staying at base camp below the dome for several days," Kimberly responded.

"I guess we're doing this last pitch one more time," Mike said to Mark. "Do you have me on belay?"

Mark looked at Mike's wrapped arm. "You're amazing!" he said. "And you are on belay."

"I'm amazing? You're the one climbing Half Dome using just your arms," Mike responded. "Climbing."

"Climb on," Mark replied.

Mike reached up with his good hand. He grabbed a rock and pulled himself up. Mike held his other arm to the side and continued climbing one-handed.

Mark fed Mike slack while Mike placed the rope back into the protection devices he had set up earlier. Soon, Mike was forty feet from the top. Then thirty feet. Then twenty feet. The cheers from the crowd grew louder with each move he made.

"You can do it, Mike!" James encouraged.

Mike extended his good arm as high as he could. "Ahhh!" he called out as his fingers just barely reached to the lip of the dome. "Come on!" he urged himself.

The crowd of onlookers grew quiet.

Mike pulled himself up slowly. He got his arm above the edge and worked his body up farther. Mike rested a moment on his stomach while his legs still dangled over the edge. He took a deep breath and hoisted the rest of his body up onto Half Dome and collapsed flat onto the ground. Mike lay there, still, for a moment.

"He looks like you did on top of Ranger Rock," Morgan whispered to James.

"I hope he's okay," Mom said.

The family joined the crowd of onlookers and approached Mike.

Mike rolled over and managed to smile. "How do I look?" he joked. His clothes were tattered, his hair was matted, and his unshaven face was covered with dirt and small cuts. Mike's wrapped arm had a large spot of blood on it, and the parts of his hands not covered with silver duct tape were caked with a combination of dirt and climbing chalk. "Not very good, I imagine."

"You look pretty good for seven days on the rock," James acknowledged.

"Yeah, seven long days," Mike said. Then he recognized James. "What a coincidence! We got here at the same time!"

Mike crawled away from the edge and began anchoring in. A crew member approached him. "We should take a look at your arm."

"Give me a few minutes," Mike responded. He turned himself around and peered down to Mark, who was still dangling next to the cliff. "I'm anchoring in now, buddy!"

Morgan looked at Mike's wounds. "What happened?"

"There was a rockfall several hours ago," Mike responded. "And we were right underneath it. The big rocks just missed us, though," Mike added. "We're lucky to be alive."

Mike peered down at Mark. "You're all anchored in now. Climb on."

"Climbing," Mark called out from below.

"That must have been what we heard this morning," Mom recalled.

Morgan, James, Mom, and Dad watched Mike haul up his gear. A crew member stepped over.

"Here, let me help you."

"I got it," Mike replied. "I want to finish what we started." He grimaced as he slowly tugged on the heavy rope attached to a bag of gear.

The other rope that was anchored at the top was pulled tightly. It wiggled and quivered as if a large fish were on the other end of the line. The crowd waited in anticipation for Mark to reach the top.

James and Morgan inched closer to the edge to watch.

Mark leaned back and took a deep breath. He let go of his pull-up bar and looked at his bulging but fatigued muscles. "Nine thousand pull-ups, thunder and lightning, rain, a snowstorm, and a rockfall later," he announced to no one in particular, "and I'm exhausted." Mark thrust the bar up and lifted his body another six inches. The gear locked in place. He thrust the bar up again and again. Mark was twenty feet from the top of Half Dome.

"Come on, Mark!" James shouted down.

Mark managed to smile. His legs dangled and tapped against the rock. Mark stopped for a moment and shook out his arms. He looked down at the 2,000-foot drop and the view all the way to Yosemite Valley. "I'm going to miss you," he said to his home for the last seven days. "But not that much!"

Mark took a deep breath. He looked up. The large crowd was watching. Morgan and James were in front.

"Here he comes!" Morgan shouted. Mark thrust his bar and hoisted himself up another six inches. Again and again he moved closer to the top. The crowd cheered each time Mark inched closer to the end. With ten feet left, he stopped again to rest his arms. "I'm exhausted," he said to everyone. "Is Kimberly up there?"

Mark pushed the bar and pulled himself up one more time.

His gear locked in place. Mark reached up and grabbed the top of Half Dome. He pulled his body over the edge and used his arms to scoot away from the cliff.

The crowd gave him a long and loud ovation.

With his hands shaking, Mark quickly freed himself from his gear. He raised his fist in the air as a salute of triumph. "Woo-hoo!" he shouted.

Mike and Mark gave each other a high five.

Kimberly rushed up to Mark. She threw her arms around him and gave him a big kiss. Mark looked at his girlfriend. "It is *so* good to see you!" he said. People started coming up to Mark and congratulating him.

Someone brought over Mark's wheelchair. "You hauled that up here?" Mark asked while hoisting himself in.

A crew member opened a small ice chest. "Hauling the wheelchair up here couldn't have been nearly as difficult as climbing the dome," he commented. He handed Mark a bottle of sparkling cider.

"You remembered!" Mark said. "Thanks."

Mark popped open the bottle. He poured some over his head and then into a glass. While the drink fizzed away, Mark raised his glass. "I want to thank all of you: my crew, my friends, my sponsors, and my girlfriend, Kimberly. Without all of you and my partner, Mike, I wouldn't have been able to do this."

Mike glanced up from the medic who was treating him. He smiled and waved.

Mark looked at the crowd. "And thank you for cheering us on," he said. "That was an extremely difficult climb. We needed every bit of your support."

Mark recognized James in the crowd. "You got hit by a rock, too, on Ranger Rock."

"But we both finished our climbs anyway!" James exclaimed.

"Yes, we did," Mark agreed.

"Would you mind if we took a picture with you?" Morgan asked.

"Of course not," Mark answered. "Just as long as you remember that I'm not in the best condition for a photo right now."

Morgan handed Mom her camera. She and James walked over to Mark. They stood on either side of him. Mom took the picture.

While Morgan was putting her camera away, Mark asked her, "Would you mind taking a picture for me in a minute?"

"Sure," Morgan responded.

Mark glanced up at Kimberly and smiled.

"You see," Mark explained, "seven days on Half Dome was the hardest thing I've ever done. But I wanted to prove to myself, and to all non-able-bodied climbers, that handicapped people can do the same things as everyone else. But I had another reason for finishing the climb."

Mark reached into the pocket of his tattered pants. He fumbled around until he pulled out a tiny jewelry box.

"Kimberly," Mark said.

Morgan now realized what Mark was doing. She got her camera ready.

Mark opened the box and pulled out a diamond ring. "You're also the reason I made it up that rock. You're my inspiration. So, Kimberly," Mark slipped the ring over his girlfriend's finger, "will you marry me?"

Morgan started snapping pictures.

Kimberly looked at Mark. A huge smile spread across her face. She leaned forward and gave Mark a big kiss. "Yes, I will!" she answered.

The crowd clapped and cheered for the newly engaged couple.

People popped open more sparkling cider and passed food around. The celebration was on.

"I can e-mail you the pictures," Morgan said.

"That would be great," Mark replied. He scratched down his e-mail address on a piece of paper.

"A proposal on Half Dome!" Mom exclaimed. "Who would have thought?"

"Maybe we should let them continue to celebrate in private," Dad suggested. "Let's have our own feast, okay?"

The Parkers found a group of rocks to sit on. They pulled out their food and water and started eating lunch.

"Lucky us, to get here right when Mark and Mike reached the top," Morgan said.

"I wonder how Mark's going to get down," Dad said.

"I wonder how we're going to get down," James said.

"Are you nervous about that?" Dad asked.

"A little," James admitted.

Morgan got up. She walked over to the snowfield and started rolling the wet, dirty snow into a ball. James joined her. Mom found some small rocks to make a face with. Dad came over and patted down the snowman to make it stable and firm. The snowman glistened in the sun.

"Pretty cool!" James said.

"We should take a picture," Mom suggested.

The family gathered around their small snowman. Morgan set the camera on a rock and pressed the automatic timer. She hurried over to join her family. The camera clicked.

"I wonder how long it will last," Morgan said.

"We'll never know," James concluded, "because we'll be long gone!"

Morgan, James, Mom, and Dad wrapped up their picnic. They packed up and looked around at the top of Half Dome once more. Mark, Kimberly, and the crew were talking, laughing, and eating. Mike was standing with his arm in a sling and talking to someone with a video camera.

The family walked over to the edge of the dome.

Once they got to the cables, Dad stopped. "It's all downhill from here!" he joked. He gripped both cables tightly and started lowering himself down.

Morgan, James, and Mom followed Dad.

For the first few steps, they held onto each cable and walked down. Then, abruptly, the pitch became very steep.

Dad stopped and peered down. "Let's see how this works." He leaned back and gripped both cables tightly. Dad turned his feet sideways and carefully sidestepped from one wooden plank to the next. Once he arrived at a plank, Dad planted his feet against the wood and called back, "That wasn't too bad."

Morgan followed Dad. She gripped one cable with both hands. Morgan slowly stepped down the rock, letting the cable slide through her hands. She joined Dad. "It looks harder than it is."

James went next. At first, he tried to scoot down with his bottom on the rock. "It's hard to hold onto the cables and do that," James said. "Maybe I'll try it your way." He then copied Morgan.

Mom sidestepped down just like Dad.

"How is it up there?" a climber asked while going up.

"It's worth every step of the way," Dad answered.

The family continued climbing down the side of Half Dome.

Farther along, Morgan moved more confidently. She let the cables slide through her hands quickly. Morgan rested on a wooden plank and turned to watch Mom and James. "This is a blast!" she said.

They passed several more groups of climbers going up. "It's interesting to see all of their expressions," James said.

"Yes. Some look happier than others," Mom replied.

"Notice how heavy they're breathing?" Morgan added.

"I wonder what we looked like when we were climbing up," James said. He guided himself down to the next plank and waited.

Soon they approached the bottom. "Almost there," Dad called out.

A moment later they slid below the last plank. Dad reached the bottom first. "Ah, level ground!" he announced.

Morgan, James, and Mom joined Dad. Morgan took a picture of everyone at the base of Half Dome with their gloves on. Then they tossed their gloves back into the pile.

"Good climbing, you two," Mom said to Morgan and James.

"That was fun!" James answered.

"It was scarier going up," Morgan stated.

Mom, Dad, Morgan, and James took one more look at the whole cable route heading up Half Dome.

"Hey!" James called out. "There's Mark."

Several crew members were carrying Mark down. Kimberly was close by. Mike was also coming down the cables, but he was only using one arm to grip them. His other arm was wrapped in the sling.

"Those two sure are tenacious," Dad said.

After traversing down the rock stairs, Morgan, James, Mom, and Dad walked much faster. They passed by the camp with the horses. People were tearing down the tents and packing up. "They must be here for Mark and Mike," Morgan concluded.

Eventually, the family made it back to Little Yosemite Valley. They took a break there. A short time later, they were at the junction to the John Muir Trail.

"Which way, James?" Mom asked.

"We can go down the way we came up," James answered, "or go left here. That will take us above Nevada Falls and back to the valley on the John Muir Trail."

"What do you think?" Dad asked.

"The John Muir Trail is a little longer," James explained.

"But we'll get to see new things," Morgan pleaded.

"Are you all feeling up to it?" Dad asked.

"I want to walk where John Muir walked!" James answered.

"I wonder if Stickeen was with him here," Morgan added.

"Can we name our puppy Stickeen?" James asked.

"Seriously?" Mom responded.

"Now that's a name that should finally *stick*," Morgan joked.

"I agree," Dad said. "Stickeen he is, then!"

The family turned left on the John Muir Trail. A moment later, they approached the footbridge above the Merced River as it plunged toward Nevada Falls a few feet away. It was crowded there, with dozens of people gazing at the falls.

Morgan, James, Mom, and Dad found an overlook. A railing protected them from a sheer 600-foot drop. Morgan took pictures. They stood at the edge, watching tumultuous curtains of white water cascade and crash on the rocks below.

"This must be the waterfall capital of the world," James said.

"It's hard to imagine more impressive ones than here," Mom agreed.

Morgan pointed far below them. "There's the pool above Vernal Falls! That's where we were this morning."

"That seems so long ago," Mom said.

Dad looked at the sky. Big billowing clouds were gathering over Yosemite's highest peaks. "It's a good thing we're not on Half Dome now," he said.

The family walked back to the main trail. They crossed the foot-bridge and continued hiking down to the valley. They zigzagged down the switchbacks on the John Muir Trail, passing mossy seeps, trickles, small streams, and wildflowers.

James took a look back at Nevada Falls and the view beyond. "'Climb the mountains and get their good tidings and cares will drop off you like autumn leaves,'" he quoted.

Dad stopped in his tracks. "You've been reading my John Muir book!"

"'How glorious a greeting the sun gives the mountains,'" Morgan added.

Mom smiled. "It looks like there are two new John Muir fans in the world. How about this one: 'In every walk with nature, one receives far more than he seeks.'"

"I sure agree with that," Dad said.

They resumed walking.

The trail worked its way back to the footbridge below Vernal Falls.

They stopped to look at the falls and listen to the roar of the water one more time.

"I'm going to miss this place!" James said.

"Me too," Morgan added. "I know we can look at pictures, but they're never the same as being here."

Morgan, James, Mom, and Dad stood at the footbridge and gazed at Vernal Falls for a few more minutes.

"It's burned into my memory now," Dad said.

The family finished the last mile of hiking down to Yosemite Valley.

WATERFALLS

Yosemite has some of the most spectacular and tallest waterfalls in the world. Here are the heights of some of Yosemite's most famous waterfalls:

Yosemite Falls—2,425 feet

This is the tallest waterfall in North America and the fifth tallest in the world.

Vernal Falls—317 feet

Illilouette Falls—370 feet

Nevada Falls—594 feet

Bridalveil Falls—620 feet

Tueeulala Falls—800 feet

Wapama Falls—1,341 feet

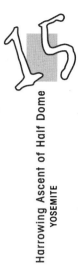

Morgan, James, Mom, and Dad sat around the campfire.

It was dark out, and hundreds of twinkling stars peeked down through the trees from the night sky.

James put another marshmallow on his coat hanger and held it over the fire. A small flame flicked up its side. The marshmallow burned lightly. James blew it out. He held the coat hanger close to his mouth and inhaled the whole marshmallow in one swallow.

"How many is that now?" Morgan asked.

"I'm not counting," James answered. "But they sure taste good after all that hiking we did today."

"I'll say," Dad said. He leaned over and held his marshmallow closer to the fire. "My muscles are so sore," he said. "I can't believe I'm the only one who feels that way."

"Speaking of sore muscles, I wonder how Mark and Mike are doing," Morgan said.

"Maybe we'll read about it in the news," Mom said.

"Are we still taking the bus up to Glacier Point tomorrow?" James asked.

"We have the tickets," Mom answered. "We just have to make sure we're all packed up in time to meet the bus."

"What time is that?" Morgan asked.

"The bus leaves at 10:30," Mom answered.

"But that's tomorrow," Dad said. "It's nice to get a chance to just sit and relax now." He adjusted his position in the chair. "Can you pass me that bag of marshmallows?"

Morgan handed the bag to Dad.

"Can I show you something?" James asked.

"Sure," Mom answered.

James unfolded his Yosemite Park map and turned on his headlamp. Mom and Dad moved their chairs closer to James. Morgan got up and stood behind him.

"What's up?" Dad asked.

"Since we're taking the bus up to Glacier Point," James explained, "Morgan and I thought it would be more fun to hike back down to the valley."

"Yeah," Morgan added. "One more hike, on the Panorama Trail."

Mom and Dad looked at each other and smiled.

James and Morgan looked at Mom and Dad.

Dad sighed. "Well … ," he started to say.

"You know," Mom began and then laughed.

"We were thinking the same thing!" Dad finally admitted. "We were just hesitant to ask. We thought you both might be too tired."

"But if we're all up for it," Mom continued, "one last hike in Yosemite would be great."

"Yes!" Morgan said.

Later that night, James climbed into his tent. He slithered into his sleeping bag, pulled out his journal, and wrote.

This is James Parker reporting.

Today we climbed to the top of Half Dome! It was scary, but also exciting. I'm amazed we did it. I think that is something I'll remember for the rest of my life. And I know I will be back to do it again.

I think when I get older, I'll get some climbing gear and maybe Morgan and I can stay at Camp 4 with all the other rock climbers.

How do I come up with a top ten list for a place like Yosemite? I know I could put a lot more than ten great sights, but here's my attempt.

James's Top Ten Sights for Yosemite

1. Yosemite Falls

2. El Capitan

3. Half Dome

4. Mist Trail

5. Bridalveil Falls

6. The Meadows and Merced River in Yosemite Valley

7. Mariposa Sequoia Grove

8. Wapama Falls

9. Hetch Hetchy Reservoir

10. Valley View Tunnel

I realize I might have to change this after we go to Glacier Point tomorrow. But that's all for now.

Reporting from Yosemite,

James Parker

Morgan tossed and turned in her sleeping bag. She sat still and listened for sounds outside her tent.

Somewhere far away in the campground, a pot banged. Then several pots clanged together. Suddenly, a car alarm sounded. The siren blared on and off.

Morgan sat up and listened.

She heard a car door open. The alarm was silenced. "Bear!" a person yelled. "Get out of here!"

Morgan heard more pots clanking. "James! Do you hear that?"

"Yes," James answered from his tent. "I wonder where it is."

"Bear!" the person shouted again.

Is that the same bear I saw? Morgan wondered.

It got quiet. Morgan listened to see if anything else was going on. She peeked out of her tent and looked around.

"I can't see any bears out there," Morgan told James. She lay back down on her sleeping bag and drifted toward sleep.

There was a distant, muffled sound of shuffling feet.

Morgan sat up. There was a lot of talking, but Morgan couldn't make out what was being said. Morgan then heard what sounded like large, heavy doors opening and closing.

She turned on her flashlight and shone it outside. Whatever was going on was too far away for Morgan to see.

Two truck engines started up, but Morgan didn't hear the trucks drive away.

Morgan got up and opened up her tent. She stepped outside and hurried over to James's tent.

"What do you think's happening?" Morgan asked James.

"I don't know," James answered.

"I have to go to the bathroom," Morgan said. "Can you make sure there are no bears around?"

"Sure," James replied. He hopped out of his tent with his flashlight and flicked it on. "I'm on bear patrol now."

James walked with Morgan over to the bathroom and Morgan went inside.

He stood outside and shone his flashlight all around.

As Morgan washed her hands and looked into the mirror, she heard the sound of trucks getting closer. Morgan quickly dashed outside the bathroom.

James was standing near the door. "Look!" he pointed.

Two bear trap trucks drove slowly by. James shone his flashlight at the trap on the first truck. Two shiny black eyes peered out of the cage. "There's the bear!" Morgan said.

James shone his light at the trap in the second truck. A small paw was sticking out near the bottom of the cage. "There's another bear!" James said.

"I wonder where they're taking them," Morgan said as the trucks drove away. She turned to James. "Thanks for keeping an eye out for me."

"Anytime," James replied.

Morgan walked back to her tent, got into her sleeping bag, found her journal, and wrote.

Dear Diary,

It's the last night of our adventure in Yosemite. But in many ways, it feels just like the beginning. I think I might want to be a nature photographer when I grow up. I already have a ton of great pictures of the mountains, cliffs, and waterfalls of Yosemite. Anyway, I can't wait to make a slide show of all my pictures when I get home.

What are my favorite sights? That is really hard to decide. Maybe I'll just <u>start</u> with waterfalls. Here are the great ones I've seen:

1. Yosemite Falls
2. Illilouette Falls
3. Vernal Falls
4. Nevada Falls
5. Bridalveil Falls
6. Wapama Falls

7. Rancheria Falls

8. Tueeullela Falls

9. The view from the top of Half Dome

10. The whole view of the valley when we climbed Ranger Rock

I can't believe all the things we've done in Yosemite. I've learned how to rock climb better. I now know that differently-abled people can climb as good as anyone. But I want to learn more about the bears. I wonder if the trapped bears we just saw are the same ones I saw last week.

Anyway, I'm going to miss Yosemite and its cliffs, rock climbing, waterfalls, and the bears. I can't wait to come back to see more of the park, including Tuolumne Meadows and the other sequoia groves.

Peaceful Slumbers,

Morgan

Morgan closed her journal and turned off her light. She stared up at the stars through the mesh window in the ceiling of her tent.

A few yards away, James also rolled over and looked up at the night sky. "There are thousands of stars up there!" he realized.

Mom and Dad lay on their backs, snuggled in their own tent.

"It's been a great trip, huh, honey?" Dad asked.

"Yes," Mom sighed. She moved her head gently against Dad's shoulder. "And I'm so glad it isn't over."

Morgan, James, Mom, and Dad sat near the back of the bus.

The driver slowed down to make a turn. "We are now on Glacier Point Road," she announced.

The bus climbed higher. Dense groves of tall trees lined the roadway. The family stared out the windows, watching the scenery.

"It's really nice not to have to walk right now," Mom said.

"I *am* pretty sore," James admitted.

Soon they came to Summit Meadow.

"Look!" Morgan called out. "There are still patches of snow on the ground."

"We're in the high country again," Dad said.

The bus caught up to two white trucks driving slowly on the road. The bus driver slowed down. A line of cars caught up to the bus.

"I wonder what's going on up there," Mom said.

The bus driver got on the microphone. "Sorry for the slow driving," she announced, "but we're behind two bear trap trucks. A mother bear and her cub have been in the Yosemite Valley campgrounds just about every night for the past several weeks."

Morgan looked at James in the seat next to her. Then she tapped Dad on the shoulder. "I bet those are our bears!" Morgan said.

"These two bears have gotten into food several times," the driver continued. "They reportedly have damaged a car.

Rangers have monitored them, but now it's time that we try relocation. Last night they finally were able to trap them using leftover food scraps from the Awahnee Hotel. Now they're bringing the bears up here to be released in the high country."

The two trucks pulled over at a turnout just past Mono Meadow.

"There they go," James said.

As the bus drove by, Morgan looked at the cages on the trucks. But it was too dark inside to see anything. "Good-bye, bears!" she called out. "And good luck!"

A short while later, the bus slowed way down. The driver turned down a series of tight, steep switchbacks. "Hang on!" the driver called out jokingly.

They came around the last bend in the road.

"Look at that!" Dad gasped.

"We're staring right at Half Dome," James added.

"There's that patch of snow," Morgan exclaimed. "I wonder if our snowman is melted by now."

"I can't believe we actually stood on top of that yesterday," Mom said.

"I don't think anyone can really appreciate Half Dome until they've climbed it," Dad concluded.

The bus stopped at a parking lot. "Welcome to Glacier Point," the driver announced. "Take your time walking around and enjoy the views. For those of you coming back, the bus will leave here in two hours. For those of you hiking, have a great trip down and we'll see you back in the valley."

The Parkers stepped off the bus.

. . .

Morgan, James, Mom, and Dad followed the crowds along a concrete trail.

"Look down there," James called out. "There's Vernal and Nevada Falls!"

The family wandered along the footpath at Glacier Point. They gazed at the views, and Morgan took several pictures.

"You can really see from up here how glaciers carved parts of the park," Dad commented. "Look at how scoured out Tenaya Canyon is."

Ahead of them, a man in a wheelchair pushed himself along the path. A woman was walking next to him.

Morgan looked over at James.

The couple stopped and looked out toward Half Dome. Morgan and James caught up to them.

"Hi!" Morgan said to Mark and Kimberly.

Mark looked up and smiled. "Well, it's good to see you again! It's a small world, isn't it?"

Mom and Dad walked up and joined them.

"Yes, it is," Mom agreed. "How are you?"

Tenaya Canyon

"A lot better than I was yesterday. I've had a chance to shower, shave, have a great meal, and get into some clean clothes. Believe me, all that is very much appreciated."

"Aren't you tired and sore?" James asked.

"Oh, yes," Mark admitted. "But I just wanted to take a look at Half Dome again. And there's no better place to do that than from Glacier Point."

"How's Mike?" Dad inquired.

"He's pretty banged up," Mark answered. "He's got several gashes, and it appears that he did get a hairline fracture in his arm. But if I know Mike," Mark added, "he'll be back on the rock in no time."

"And you?" Morgan asked.

Mark stared out over Yosemite and thought for a moment. "I'm going to take a break for a while. But there are more mountains to climb. Mike and I have been talking about conquering El Capitan next."

"And this time I'm going with them," Kimberly added, "to be the trip photographer."

The Parkers stood and looked out at Yosemite with Mark and Kimberly.

"Well, it's great seeing you again," Morgan said.

Mark smiled. "You too."

Morgan, James, Mom, and Dad walked along the path. "I'll be right back," Dad suddenly announced.

A moment later, Dad came up holding a shopping bag.

"What did you get?" Morgan asked.

"You'll see," Dad answered.

Mom looked at Dad suspiciously.

They walked farther along the trail toward Glacier Point. A large crowd was there. Morgan, James, Mom, and Dad went right up to the concrete barrier and looked down.

"There's a swimming pool down there!" James called out.

"And more than 3,000 feet of cliff between us and it," Dad said nervously.

"There's good ol' Yosemite Falls," Morgan said.

After a few minutes at the overlook, James guided his family back toward the Panorama Trail. "Eight and a half miles to the valley floor," he announced. "Ready?"

"Wait a second," Dad said. He rummaged through his shopping bag and pulled out four T-shirts. "Go ahead and look at them," Dad said, handing out the shirts.

Morgan unfolded hers first. "I climbed Half Dome" it read. "It's perfect!"

Morgan, James, Mom, and Dad slipped their T-shirts on over the ones they were already wearing.

"You can wear those with pride," Dad said. "You've earned them. Oh, one other thing." Dad fished into his shopping bag and pulled out four ice cream sandwiches.

"I was starting to get hungry," James admitted.

"Me too," Morgan added.

They walked over to some rocks and sat down.

James smiled. "Ice cream sandwiches with a view."

Mom put her arms around her family. "Look at us," she said, smiling. "We're four enthusiastic national park explorers!"

A few minutes later, James stood up. He took the ice cream wrappers from Morgan, Mom, and Dad and threw them into a nearby bear-proof garbage can.

"Can I show you the way?" James asked. He took the first steps on the Panorama Trail. The family followed.

Quickly, the crowds at Glacier Point were left behind.

"Just look at this amazing scenery!" Dad called out. "This is the greatest hiking trail in the world!"

"Because it's the one we're on right now," Morgan added.

"Exactly!" James said.

And the family began the long descent back toward Yosemite Valley.